Love in Times of Contempt

A multicultural romance novella follow up

Leonor Soliz

Leonor Soliz

Cover Art by Leonor Soliz

Final formatting by Leonor Soliz

First edition

Paperback ISBN: 978-1-7782872-5-1

Ebook ISBN: 978-1-7782872-6-8

To everyone who finds comfort in loving domesticity. Joy is in the small moments.

Contents

Author's Note

MY BOOKS ALWAYS END in a Happily Ever After. My stories are generally fluffy, with a good mix of humor and angst. Nevertheless, I believe it's important to give readers every chance to consent to reading my book. Although I write generally happy romance, if you'd like to access content warnings for this story, check this link (ebook) or visit this page: https://leonorsoliz.com/books/love-in-times-of-contempt/.

Note 2: LITOC takes place before both epilogues for Seeking Stars.

The chronological order for everything is as follows:

SS >> LITOC >> LITOC epilogue 1 >> LITOC epilogue 2 >>

SS epilogue 2 >> SS epilogue 1

Somehow, I didn't think this would be confusing while writing it hahahaha

I hope you enjoy <3

Chapter One

ANA TOOK A BREAK from staring at her screen and rubbed her tired eyes. She massaged her lids, counting through a few deep breaths. She hadn't checked the time in a while, but based on the sudden roaring in her stomach, she'd hyperfocused on her work for too long.

With a sigh, she stretched and leaned back against her desk chair. She reached for her phone and navigated to her notifications, already thinking about what she'd make for dinner. She got distracted by texts from both Liam and Ely from some time ago.

> Liam: Sry, gonna be
> home late, maybe
> around 8. Some stuff
> happened w the flight
> sched. Can't wait to
> see you

It would be some time before he made it home, then. After a bit over a year together, she was used to all his traveling, but didn't enjoy it. She couldn't wait for Liam to be home.

> Ana: I'll wait for
> you to have dinner.
> See you soon

With a sigh, Ana checked Ely's text next.

> Ely: It's been ages since
> I've sent you a link to a
> Liam thing, but this was
> worth sharing. It's a good
> thing I think

With a preemptive smile, Ana opened the link on her computer. It took her to what seemed like an interview; a pretty blonde sat in front of Liam against a branded backdrop for his latest movie, production companies and movie logos on a black fabric. He wore a shirt she'd given him, and Ana's smile widened as she settled to watch the video.

The reporter spoke to the camera. "We're here with Liam McMillan, one of the hottest actors in the world. His new movie, *Lethal Whispers,* premiered with record-breaking numbers last week. With his fame soaring high, we're sitting with him today to learn more about his current projects and near future." She turned to him. "Hi Liam, how are you?"

"I'm excellent, thanks." His eyes sparkled under the set lights and his lips took on a slightly mischievous smile; a somersault flipped her stomach at the sight. The interviewer grinned.

"This movie is such a genre bender... action, suspense, drama... it has it all!"

"Yes, it was great. I got to flex my acting muscle a lot."

"As well as every other muscle, am I right?"

Ana chuckled at the awkward and flirty joke. The blonde giggled; Liam responded with a charming smile.

"Filming action, especially, is a very physical job."

"Do you do all your own stunts?"

"No, not all of them. Sorry to disappoint..." The glint in his eyes lacked all trace of an apology. Ana shook her head at him on principle, but a smile curved her lips.

The interviewer continued. "According to your social media, you recently went back into romance and filmed a romantic drama."

"Yeah, I did. It had been a while since I'd done that kind of movie and the script was amazing."

"The movie is based on a book, *At The End Of The World* by Luna Ferreira. Did you read the book as part of your research?"

"I did. It was lovely. The depth of emotion between the two main characters was beautiful to read, and an honor to embody."

"Oh, does that mean that you're a romantic?"

He wet his bottom lip, frowning as if thinking about the question. It didn't hide the gleam in his eye. Warmth spread through Ana's chest, as if her body could guess what he was about to say.

"I am. I'm the kind of person who wants my own happily ever after. I don't think there's anything better than having a partner whom you adore and with whom you're willing to work through the challenges of a relationship. Of life."

"That's lovely! Have you found your happily ever after?"

Ana scoffed at the journalist's question. She knew for a fact that the interviewing team would have received the same guidelines everyone did, asking to limit personal questions and make no reference to his love life.

Liam seemed to have no problem setting that boundary again. "C'mon, you know I have a standard answer for that kind of question."

"Yes—" The reporter grinned. "No comments."

"That's right."

"Well, Ana Lira is certainly a lucky lady."

Liam's lips curled up at the corners but he shook his head. Sometimes journalists tried to get him talking about it regardless, and it seemed this particular reporter was hellbent to get him to do it.

"No comments, remember?" Liam insisted.

"You can't blame me for trying." The interviewer's smile never faltered. "Tell me about the documentary. The rumor is that even though it's supposed to be about a breaking point in your career over a year ago, it also tells the story about how you two fell in love."

Ana cringed. This reporter had tried really, really hard to get him to talk about his personal life— their life together. No wonder Ely had linked her to the video. As her best friend, she continued to keep an eye on the online gossip about Ana and Liam's relationship. Ely didn't share much with Ana these days, but having a chance to see Liam shine allowed for some rule bending.

Liam frowned but left it at that. He was a professional, after all. "The official theme of the documentary is about that breaking point you're referring to. As it was publicized back then, I changed agents and redefined the future of my career as a direct result of the stress I was going through, both professionally and personally. It's a big risk to take, showing that to the world; the director and I worry about some sort of backlash, but we're hoping that our fans will appreciate how raw, honest, and vulnerable the content is."

"We for sure can't wait to see it! Thank you so much for talking to us today!"

After a few polite goodbyes, the video ended with logos and credits, as usual.

Ana opened the text app on her computer and wrote a short response to Ely.

Ana: Wow. They tried really
hard to get him to

talk about us, but
Liam held the line

Ely: Like a champ. At
least it's more publicity
for your film. He's arriving
today, right?

Ana: Yeah, he should
be here in a
few hours

Ely: Tell him
he's a champ

Ana: Lol, I will!

———

Ana worked on administrative tasks for her and Liam's new production company, music playing in the background. She worked at Liam's desk; as she'd spent more time in LA, they'd rearranged the office to have two work surfaces, one for Ana's editing hardware and another for more general laptop use. Her eyes lifted from the screen in front of her as she caught movement in the hallway.

"There you are." Liam let go of his luggage and stepped into the office.

"You're here!" Ana got up and walked around the desk, approaching him with glee in each step. "I didn't hear you arrive."

He wore a hoodie she'd given him for his birthday, and her heart pitter-pattered at the image that came with it: him choosing it to take it with him as a concrete memory of home. Of her.

God, she'd missed him.

She strode to meet him in the middle of the room, where she jumped into his arms— she was a tall-ish woman with plenty of padding around her form, but one thing she'd learned over the past year? He could hold her up.

She grinned and surrounded his neck with her arms while his hands wrapped around her thick thighs, his fingers squeezing the softness there. He patted and grabbed all the way up her legs, until he settled with firm hands on her ass. She kissed him deeply.

"You're early." She kept her lips within kissing distance. "Your text said you'd be later than this?"

"Yeah, there was a change and things actually moved faster than I thought." He kissed her once on each cheek. "And now I'm on a break. I can already feel the stress leaving my body."

She kissed him on the mouth, a silent complaint against his demure gesture. "I can't wait to *finally* meet your family this weekend."

He rolled his eyes but accompanied it with a smile. He released her and her feet found the ground again. "You too? My parents have been giving me grief over it. You know we tried several times and it just didn't work out."

Her smile widened. She lifted herself onto the balls of her feet and leaned against him; her arms remained on his shoulders. "Doesn't mean I'm not going to tease you about it."

"Do I need to remind you I've only met your parents for dinner twice?"

"Anyway," she said, her eyebrows lifting. "I prepped food earlier, but was waiting for you to come home to finish getting dinner ready. Are you hungry?"

"Ravenous." The sparkle in his eyes told her he wasn't think-ing about food. His hands found her ass again.

"Oh? Did you miss any particular home delicacies?"

"Some in particular." Not letting go of her, he walked her back until she collided against the bookcase.

"Anything that could satisfy your appetite at the moment?"

"This is something." He made a show of studying the shelves. "'Cause it just occurred to me that I haven't fucked you against these yet."

She faked hesitation, and twisted around to inspect the large piece of furniture as well. "I don't know if it'll work—"

He interrupted her by grabbing her by the thighs and lifting her to sit her on a small decorative ledge. "Your sexy ass fits perfectly here. If I remove your jeans I can make this work. Or I can bend you over and fuck you like that, too. Or both."

"Show me," she whispered, before he got down to business.

Chapter Two

LATER, AFTER LIAM FOUND a third position against the book-shelf and gave her two orgasms, they succumbed to hunger for real food. He went to take a shower while she finished dinner, all with a sore backside from the way the wood had dug into her flesh. Worth it, though.

Now Ana sat at the dinner table across from Liam; his face held a level of relaxation he never seemed to reach while on their video calls across the world.

He swallowed a big bite of the encocado de camarón she'd made. "Did you hear from Carruthers?"

How Liam could be calm, awaiting the important news from one of their lawyers, was beyond Ana. It was hard to believe that she now had access to a team of them, all with different specializations, thanks to her boyfriend. Wild.

Ana grinned. This was a piece of news she'd been wanting to share while looking at his gorgeous face. She had big plans for this conversation. "Yes, we finally have the green light. We can actually start looking for an office, prep the launch of the rebrand, et cetera."

"Yes! Finally!" He reached to hold her hand over the table. "We can really get started on this. Though I don't know how excited we're going to be as we go about hiring people."

She nodded, taking a sip of water. "I know. It's like trusting our baby to other people. But we need help, especially in the next few months."

"Yeah, we need help." He squeezed her hand again and let it go, returning to his plate. "Getting to this point was hard already, just the two of us— and Mo, with all his personal assistant superpowers— it slowed down the documentary production. We need to get this started and hire people."

Ana speared a shrimp with her fork. "Agreed. You can tell Jen to keep it all in mind when she's doing her agent-y thing, so that the flow of your projects gives you room for production tasks." She scooped some coconut milk sauce on the shrimp and took a bite.

"I'll write to her tomorrow. Should I ask Mo to put out the word that we're hiring an operations manager and a social impact manager?"

She studied him, fork resting on her plate, and gulped down the sudden nerves gripping her throat.

He stared back, a curl appearing at the corner of his mouth. "Out with it. I know you're preparing to tell me something."

A smile formed on her lips despite her apprehension. "Yeah, you're right. I've been thinking... What if we hired Ely as the social impact manager? Listen," she argued, even though she didn't see any signs that he would interrupt her. "Ely is the best at everything, you know that." He chuckled, which gave her a push to finish her plea. "She has lots of experience in the not-for-profit world, dealing with the for-profit world, and she already has expertise managing social media campaigns."

"Ely, huh?" Liam rested his fork on the plate as well, steepling his hands together, elbows on the table.

"Yes. I honestly think she'd be amazing for the job. Really. But in the spirit of full disclosure, the fact that she'd have to move here is appealing to me, too."

He laughed. "Of course it is."

"So what do you think?" She picked up her fork again, but didn't use it right away.

"Well..." Liam took his fork as well and shoveled a big bite into his mouth. Ana imitated him as he thought. "Honestly, I'm kind of excited. I've been thinking about that myself. You know I love Ely and my gut says she'd be amazing for the role. My mind says I should be more professional about this and interview her with the job in mind, though."

"You've been thinking about it? Why didn't you tell me?"

"I've been trying to think about it from different angles, and I didn't want you to get excited about it if it doesn't make sense."

Ana picked up the last of her food with the help of her knife, and savored the last bite. Hearing Liam had considered the idea himself released the last of her nerves.

"I think it makes sense. She's perfect to build what we want out of the position; she's had to wear so many hats at work before. You know how it is in the not-for-profit world, some-times."

Liam arched an eyebrow. "Do I?"

She squinted at him. "Ha. Anyway, I'm a hundred percent sure of the social impact side of things. If the social media thing felt too difficult for her, she could always outsource it. You know that's in our business model already."

"Have you talked to her about this yet?" Liam took his last bite of food and reached for his glass of water.

Ana dabbed her lips with her napkin. "No, I wanted to talk with you first."

"Thanks." He smiled. "I know it must have been hard for you not to discuss it with her."

"It was," she said, mirroring his grin. She squeezed his hand over the table this time. "But you're my partner. In business and— god, I don't know how to say this in a non-clichéd way, but you're also my partner in life."

He laughed. "I share the sentiment, if not the corny words."

She shook her head and tried to let go of his hand, but he grabbed it and linked their fingers together, his smile impish. "I'm tempted to challenge you to find a better way to say it."

"Tell me you missed me, instead."

Ana pursed her lips, considering. "I suppose I did. Maybe that's why I kept having this image in my head, the entire time you were gone. I kept thinking... Bloomington isn't the right place for me anymore."

Despite her show of nonchalance, nerves twirled in her stomach. He remained silent, but his eyes softened and a small smile appeared on his lips.

"I don't know," she continued. "I keep seeing this image in my head... this new vision for myself and for us, of course. I see Ely moving here, you and I having this project here, so much of my life here and, well... You know I still somewhat divide my time between here and Bloomington, but also— I've gone back less and less. Both places feel like home, but living here with you... that's what feels right."

He said nothing, but moved his chair back and pulled at her hand. Understanding his intention, she walked around the table and sat sideways on his lap.

Her arms went around his neck, his around her waist, holding her close.

His eyes sparkled as he gazed at her. "You living with me here feels right. Making it official and all."

She nodded. "Whether you agree to hire Ely or not, this is something I'd like to do. Whether she moves here or not, I want to be here with you."

Liam kissed her. "I love you, Ana. Please move in with me. Permanently."

"So you don't think a year is too little time?" She dropped her forehead to his as she voiced her one doubt.

"Of course not. You know I've been ready for a while."

"Yeah, you're often ready before me in this relationship." She kissed one of his temples, then the other.

He closed his eyes, enjoying her affection. "As long as you catch up, I'll wait for you."

"You're seriously amazing, Liam."

"And you're going to love me even more if we end up hiring Ely, aren't you?"

She laughed. She kissed his lips again. "My love for you isn't conditional on that."

"Good. But we should call her. See if she'd be interested at all."

Ana's smile grew, delighted at the idea of surprising Ely. Ana helped Liam clear the table and got drinks as he loaded the dishwasher, before settling on the sofa to call her.

"How much does she know about the details we've planned for Jump Cannon?" Liam asked as Ana unlocked her phone.

"Not much. A while ago, she and I decided I wasn't going to tell her much about Jump Cannon's social aspect, so that you and I could come up with our plan first without pressure from her experience. Her words. This will surprise her."

Ana navigated to her starred contacts and video called Ely, who responded on the third ring.

"Hello? Give me a sec." Ely's hair filled the screen as she finished doing whatever she'd been doing; Ana snuggled close to Liam on the couch. With a quick flick, Ely's face filled the screen. "Hey, what's up?"

"I'm moving in with Liam," Ana replied, jumping into the conversation as usual.

"She is." Liam put his arm around Ana and brought her closer to him.

"Pfffft," Ely scoffed. "Old news. You've been living there for months and visiting your old crew here once in a while, especially the last six months."

"Fair, but that wasn't official." Ana brought her hair forward, freeing it from under Liam's arm. "It's official now. I'm breaking my lease, selling my stuff, bringing whatever's left."

"So you're going to finally leave me?" Ely sighed. "Liam, you know I adore you, but this pisses me off a little."

Ana raised her eyebrows. "I thought we've made it work? We text every day and talk on the phone five times a week."

"Sure, but I also lived with the certainty you'd come by and I'd get to hug you every couple of months. I'm sure moving there means you'll come here less often."

"How old is your resume?" Liam asked. "Send it to me and we can see if there's something here we can offer to you."

"Okay, I forgive you if you apologize by getting me a job there. I'm open to relocating, especially now that Ana is going to be there. My parents will survive it; they did when I moved out."

Ana laughed. "And what can they really do? Your parents and mine— they like to complain about our choices all the time. We're so gringas, you know."

"Exactly," Ely agreed, "but some of these choices you're making are to move your relationship forward. Your parents are going to like that. Me? Moving away from family for work?"

"No, for family, too." Ana arched an eyebrow. "We're sisters."

Ely's mouth took on a sassy smile. "They might still renounce us, you know."

"Sooo... should we look into getting you to move here?" Liam's eyes jumped from Ana to Ely on the screen.

"For sure!" Ely's voice was full of conviction. "Eventually we'll just convince our parents to move to LA, too. For now, let's talk options. My resume is a couple years old, since the last time I changed jobs; I'll send it to you. Do you know a lot of people in the not-for-profit world, Liam?"

"Depends what kind of job you'd want. Do you think you could handle a job organizing a social impact department?"

Ely's eyes opened wide. "Oooh, someone you met through your company? What's the vision?"

"Helping connect underprivileged and underrepresented youth and young adults with volunteering, training, and shadowing opportunities within the filming industry." Ana bit the inside of her cheek not to reveal their intentions.

"Are you kidding? That's my area." Ely stopped for a second, her eyes turning dreamy. "Youth and young adults are my favorite population, and creating those opportunities for them would be incredible. Talk about inspiring representation! Social justice and equity work, it just... it'd be brilliant, honestly. It'd be the next step in my career. I can already see it. It could be amazing! Where do I send my resume?"

"I mean, you don't know all the details." A chuckle escaped Ana. "There's also a social media aspect to the job; the social impact side will be showcased within the company, so creating relevant content online— which will have to also add some of the production projects for publicity and to entice participants— managing that will be part of the job."

Ely dismissed it with a shake of her head. "Multitasking and multiple roles are typical in my world. I've done a lot of content creating in the past and you both know I'm comfortable online. Besides, creating content could be shaped to be one of the internships for a youth applicant. I'd probably want to network with someone who handles content creation for social media, to fine tune the profile. I'll create a personal account to lurk around and get exposed to the typical content in the niche, to come to my interview with some good ideas. I can also present a mock up project about how a young participant may shadow a producer or something..."

"That sounds great," Ana said. "I knew you'd rock a job like this one."

"I would, and you both know I don't do false modesty," Ely added. "I think I would be a great fit. Is this someone you met while working on your production company? I know you guys also want to add a social impact side and, really, you should consider doing something like this, when the company finally gets the green light. Anyway, I want to get that job. Do you know what kind of interview process it is? Send me the info so I can prep my resume, cover letter, and interview."

"Okay, you're really into it, aren't you?" Ana asked, a smile breaking on her face.

She looked at Liam to gauge his reaction, and the grin that echoed hers sparked hope inside of her.

"I so am. This would be a great opportunity, even if it weren't in LA with my bestie. So do me a solid and look into how to prep for that interview to max my chances—"

"Send it to admin at Jump Cannon dot film," Liam said.

"You want me to send it to you? Isn't Jump Cannon your company?"

"Yes. We need to document due diligence, but it wouldn't be fair to call for other resumes if they're not likely to compete with you. You have an edge, because we obviously think it's a great idea to work with people you're close with and you really seem incredible for the role."

Ana kissed Liam on the cheek in excitement.

"Excuse me?" Ely asked, confusion clear in her voice.

"Sorry, I didn't even get a chance to explain anything!" Liam continued. "You jumped into it so hard that I have no option but to be in awe at what just happened."

"And what *did* just happen?" Ely asked. "Because it can't... you can't... I mean—"

"You do it," Liam said to Ana.

"No." Ely insisted. "Are you serious?"

"No?" Liam asked, but there was humor in his voice.

"I mean, yes! Fuck it, just say it. For real?"

"How would you like to work for Jump Cannon, Ely? I told Liam I think you're perfect for the role and wow, you delivered."

"Ely," Liam added, "we want you to apply to the role of Social Impact Manager at Jump Cannon Productions. We really think you'd be the perfect fit. This call had everything I would have wanted to hear from a candidate for the role during an interview, and you hadn't even prepared."

For the first time in Ana's life, Ely didn't fill the space with words right away.

"Ely?"

"She's in shock," Liam guessed.

"She's never speechless, though," Ana said. "This is very weird. Did you get what we said, Ely? Unless you committed a crime I don't know about and your criminal record ruins your secret— in which case you'd have so much to explain, Elena Castillo— we're offering you a job."

Silence still filled the line.

"Unless you don't want it?" Liam asked.

"Just give me a sec— I just—" Ely tried.

"Do you need to think about it?" Liam offered, but she interrupted him.

"No! I don't need to think about it. I was just going through my mental list of things I need to do— quit my job, pack, sell, move..."

"So is that a yes?" Ana wanted to confirm.

"It's such a loud, unconditional, and resolute yes you'll hear it all the way over there, my friends."

"We'll get our lawyer to send you everything soon." Liam squeezed Ana close. "For now, this is goodnight from me. I have therapy early tomorrow."

"And I'm assuming Ana is going to bed with you, after this time apart," Ely added. "I'll go to bed soon myself. I'll have plenty of daydreams about my life in California to keep me up at night, if I'm not careful."

Chapter Three

"IT'S SO NICE TO see you, Doc." Liam sat on the worn leather sofa and got comfortable, a to-go cup of coffee from home in his hand.

Dr. Linda smiled. "You too, it's been a while."

"Yeah, how long? A month and a half?"

"Or so, yes." Dr. Linda adjusted her glasses with a gesture so familiar to Liam that he smiled. "Last time we met, you were still waiting to hear about the documentation for the production company."

He grinned. "Yes, we finally got the green light, and we even hired our first employee."

She clapped her hands together. "Wonderful!"

"We hired Ely, Ana's best friend."

"Oh, yes. You've mentioned her before."

"Yeah. I think she could do great things for the company." Liam sipped from his drink.

Dr. Linda nodded. "You've put a lot of hope in it; it makes sense to me that you want to make sure you choose the right people."

Velvety coffee warmed its way down his throat. "Exactly, and I think Ely is a good bet."

"So now you're in business with Ana and her best friend. Are you still comfortable with the whole thing?"

Liam would have thought that Dr. Linda had doubts, if he didn't know her well after two years of working together. Linda's number one goal was to help him gauge whether his emotions and thoughts aligned as he made decisions throughout his life. He took her question at face value.

"Yep. Everything is still going well." He traced the texture of the cup's plastic sleeve with a finger as he talked. "The company stuff is gaining momentum. I'm not that worried about working with Ana and her best friend; I wouldn't have offered to invest in Ana's production company in the first place if I had worried it's a bad idea. I think it's neutral, really, and Ana— well, she tells me it's pretty common in her culture to work with family and friends."

"As long as boundaries are clear, I also think it can be neutral. Especially if you and Ana are still doing well."

"And we are." He smiled. "I swear, Linda, Ana's just what I'd been looking for."

Amusement appeared in the slant of her mouth. "I believe you! I promise. Every time we talk about her, you light up like the skies parted and the only ray of sunlight for miles fell on you alone."

He chuckled. "That's how it feels."

"I'm happy for you, Liam." Her eyes softened as she looked at him. "You worked hard, you waited for a while, and at the end you found what you wanted."

"I did." A smile stretched over his face. "She's moving in with me; officially."

"That's great! Congratulations."

"Thank you." He had to stop his chest from puffing up, like he'd gotten an award for being good at relationships now.

"Any big fights yet?"

He laughed. The contrast in their train of thought was not lost to him. "Nope. Not yet."

"They'll come eventually." She pulled at something on her skirt he could not see. "And each time you have one and choose each other, your relationship will grow stronger."

"In theory, I guess. But why would we fight? Beyond the little annoyances of the everyday, anyway."

She lifted a shoulder. "It could be anything. Old patterns resurfacing or something completely different. It doesn't matter. Just be prepared, and do your best. You have the right skills already."

"But wouldn't the skills mean there are fewer reasons to fight?" He frowned.

"Oh, not at all! You're still human, Liam. Having the skills means that when fights do happen, they'll be healthier fights."

"Huh." His eyebrows arched high for a second before he smirked. "I'm sure there'll be a session at some point when we get to talk about that fight you predict. For now, though— Ana and I are good."

"That really is amazing. And with that, your romantic life and work life are finally balanced."

"They are— mostly. Work still needs to slow down a bit but— yeah. It's all good."

Dr. Linda squinted ever so slightly, keeping quiet for a couple of seconds.

Liam closed his eyes and sighed. "Oh, no. You have that look. You found what you want to talk about."

She laughed. "You got me. I want to talk about your brother."

"Alex? Why?" He groaned.

"Because it's the one part that feels unresolved for you. Right? Every time we talk about him, you get a bit irritated with me."

Liam took a deep breath and held it in his lungs for a few seconds. He loved Alex, and wanted him close. They'd grown up like best friends, doing everything together, with lots of fighting included. While those got resolved when they were kids... they'd grown apart as they became adults.

Attempts had been made, on Liam's part, to figure things out and try to be close again, but Alex had pushed back with his brand of grump, and kept Liam at arm's length.

Liam frowned. "Well, that's because I don't think it should fall on me to make things better between us. I've tried already."

"Who said it falls on you?"

"I guess you haven't said so, really."

Liam was older than Alex by about two years; the difference hadn't really seemed to affect their relationship growing up, but maybe it was okay to blame his impulse to fix things with Alex on some unconscious sense of responsibility as the older brother. A potentially misguided sense of it.

"No, I haven't said so." She raised an eyebrow. "I just want to know how you are feeling about your relationship with Alex."

"Frustrated, as always." Liam took a big gulp of coffee and shook his leg. "He responds to half my texts and a quarter of my calls. When we do talk, most of the time he's short tempered. I really don't know what else I'm supposed to do."

"Has he told you why he keeps you at such a distance?"

"Not lately." He shook his head.

"Have you asked?"

He had, a couple of times in recent years. Each time, Alex had looked at Liam with scorn, shaken his head, and given him some sort of excuse.

Annoyed, Liam took another sip and stared at the ceiling. "Not lately."

Dr. Linda hid a smile. "So what has he said in the past?"

"Last thing he said was that he didn't want to live in the halo of Hollywood; that if we're close it makes it worse."

"Do you believe him?"

He shrugged and brought his eyes down to the doctor again. "I'm sure it's part of it."

"But what does your gut tell you?"

Liam traced the cup sleeve once more, taking his time to answer. A big part of therapy had been to learn to trust his gut again, and a childish part of him didn't want to use this hard-earned skill on his brother.

"We could talk about why you don't want to talk about Alex." Dr. Linda's voice held a hint of mischief. While Liam typically appreciated her humor, right now, her suggestion wasn't that funny to him. It was even worse.

Talking about Alex meant not talking about himself, giving Liam a reprieve from confronting where his irritation for Alex came from.

Liam locked his gaze on Dr. Linda and answered with the truth. "I think there's something else going on with Alex. That's what my gut is telling me. I know he hates his job and he hasn't been able to paint for a while... but that can't be it, can it?"

Dr. Linda followed his mood tone. "I can't know for sure as he's not my client and I only know him through you but, in general terms, I don't see why that can't be it."

"What do you mean?" He tracked all the tiny movements on her face.

"If painting means a lot to him, not being able to paint could really affect him. All of this is just guessing on our part, just me trying to help you understand your own perspective of him. If you think his irritability has to do with his painting, then it could very well be the case."

"I guess." Liam frowned. "I know he wanted to paint more."

"You've said you do like acting. Right?"

Liam nodded. "Yeah. And I think I know where you're going with this. If I suddenly couldn't act anymore, it'd rock my world— in a bad way."

"So, if you consider that, and empathize with Alex a bit; and if you think about what it's like to do something you hate to do... what happens when you think of Alex?"

Liam took his therapist's words in and let himself engage with them. He searched through his mental files, picking up images of Alex's paintings hanging in Liam's home, and how the color and shape of them invariably plucked a chord in Liam's soul; he imagined what it took to translate emotion and vision into a painting... and what it might feel like to lose the language of it. It left a hollow cavity behind, just to think about.

Liam missed Alex. Last time they'd met, his brother's eyes had been shuttered, and the memory came with sorrow. Perhaps it was an echo of what might be living in Alex's heart.

Liam sighed. "I think he's going through a rough time."

"And how does that make you feel?"

"I feel bad for him." He shrugged off the discomfort tensing his shoulders. "But I'm making this up! I don't know what he's actually feeling, or why he's still working there."

"I could be wrong, but to me it seems there's something about this situation that really upsets you, and it makes you angry. Is it because you don't understand him, or because Alex won't talk to you about it, or something else?"

Liam shook his head. "I'm not sure, Doc. Generally I'm too pissed off to look too closely."

She chuckled. "Well, that's fair. That's one of the things anger does. But you want to figure it out, don't you? Or is the anger too big?"

Coffee seemed like the right thing to gain more time. He drank a bit more. "Anger's big, but I do want to figure it out."

"You always have a choice, even about that." Dr. Linda gave him one of her encouraging smiles. "Maybe you realize you actually are okay doing nothing; maybe you confirm you do want to try again. Then you can keep thinking about how to be his brother, if he's going through a rough time."

"Dammit, Doc. I should be used to admitting this but, I guess that makes sense."

Dr. Linda's smile turned cheeky. "When will you see him again?"

Liam scoffed. "Tonight, actually. Ana and I are going to my parents' house for a visit. We're driving out of LA in a couple of hours."

She took a sip of water from the glass she always kept nearby, then nodded. "See how it feels, and consider asking him about his painting if you like. Only he can tell you what's going on."

"He'll just tell me to mind my own business."

"If you care enough about mending your relationship with him, then give him the opportunity to prove you wrong. At the very least, you'll be showing him you care about how he's doing, and that you're open to talking with him, if he's willing to open up."

Chapter Four

A FEW HOURS AFTER Liam's return from therapy, Ana sat in his car while he found some music to put on the stereo for their trip. The gate to his house— their house? When was she supposed to start calling it their place?— took the journey to automatically close behind them.

"So, we're gonna be living together soon." Ana adjusted her sunglasses on the bridge of her nose, and Liam got the car moving in the direction of San Luis Obispo. "The house is yours, of course, but if it's going to be our home... should I start paying some of the bills? More than I have to date with food and stuff. Once I move out from my old place I won't have to keep it going, so I could relocate my bills here."

After a year in the neighborhood, Ana recognized most of the houses around, and could even spot her favorite ornamental flowers in front of some of them.

"Sure, we should look at the expenses and see what you can take over." He shoulder-checked as he changed lanes. "Just don't suggest we split expenses in the middle, okay?"

Ana snorted. "I won't suggest that because I don't think I could afford it, but I'd like to do a bit."

"We can look into that." He stole a look at her. "You won't feel weird about my money now, will you?"

"No, not really." She shrugged. "I'd like to do my part on the practical and financial aspects of being together and living together, but since you have more money, you can pay more. We can keep it proportional. I can keep my independence. I'll get a salary from Jump Cannon and my films and I can keep my own bank account; pay for what I need. Though of course you can use your money to give me expensive gifts once in a while if you'd like."

He chuckled. "Is that a suggestion?"

The views changed fast. Big, fancy houses gave way to more dense buildings, and soon Liam drove them through busy city roads.

The intermittent sound of the blinkers filled the car as they waited to turn.

Ana smiled. "I mean, couples gift things to each other, right? I might not be able to afford the kind of gifts you could give me, but I'll be giving you things, too."

The car moved again, and Liam did that thing turning the wheel with the palm of his hand that, for some reason, looked so damn hot. "I was thinking of getting you a car."

Heat disappeared, replaced by a sudden cool stillness inside of her. "A car?"

"I travel so much that we haven't had a lot of problems sharing this one, but now that your whole life will happen here, better to have two. No?"

"Uhm. Right." She gulped. "I was thinking like, earrings for a party. A car feels so... settled."

They reached one of the last traffic lights before getting on the freeway; Ana stared at the crimson glass, without blinking, until her eyes glazed over.

A few seconds had probably ticked by. Liam's voice held a careful tone. "And is that a problem?"

"No. Of course not." Ana blinked sense into herself again. "I should probably get used to stuff like that."

The light changed and they gained speed, silence between them for a minute. Something big was building in this conversation.

Liam drummed the fingers of one hand against the wheel. "What about five years from now? Ten? Will we keep separate accounts forever?"

Ana stared at him, studying his face. "Uhm... you want to make decisions about that today? We don't know if anything's gonna change in five years."

"Change like... what?" He frowned, the wrinkles at the top of his nose barely visible in his profile.

He flicked the blinkers on again as he approached the merge with the freeway.

Ana shrugged, eyes still on him. "Finances. How we separate things."

"Oh, I see." He seemed to take a deep breath. "It's just that at some point you may have rights over my stuff. Or vice versa. Might make more sense to have a joint account as well."

Her eyes opened wide, and her lungs appeared to suffer a mild dysfunction. "Wait. I could have rights to your stuff? Is that a thing in California? Even for people who aren't married?"

The car settled into a steady pace among the other traveling vehicles.

He stole a quick glance at her. "I don't know, actually. I never thought about this stuff before."

"Right." She faced forward and stared out the windshield. A chill ran down her back. "I guess we should look into that."

"Okay." He cleared his throat. "Then we should probably talk to a lawyer about it. When do you think is a good time?"

Ana blinked for a long moment, her heart beating faster than she'd thought. For reasons she didn't understand. "What do you mean?"

"Should I ask for a referral for a lawyer now? In another year?"

"Oh." She grabbed her water bottle from the console and gulped some of it. "I don't know. I think it's like asking, when do we know for sure we'll stay together for long enough that it's worth doing all of that? How do we know when we've crossed that milestone? I want to be with you forever, but do I *know* we will be? Not really. We're still in the honeymoon phase."

"Mmh," Liam said. "To you this is about having concrete proof we'll be permanent, knowing if we'll be together when we're eighty."

"I gather it's not the same to you?"

Ugh. The conversation was going fast, and her attention refused to inspect her discomfort, and instead zeroed in on Liam. Like he had all the answers.

He seemed focused on the road, but his continuing frown told her he was paying close attention to their conversation, too.

He shrugged, his hands still firmly placed on the steering wheel. "No, I see it as a practical step to make sure we're keeping things in order. We agreed we're making choices based on the assumption that we'll stay together. I assume we'll be together when we're eighty."

Crap, her lungs seemed to reject the oxygen in the air. "If we're being practical, then... in that case, we might as well talk to a lawyer sooner rather than later, I think? To see what to expect."

"Okay." He nodded. "I'll ask Carruthers to give us a referral to someone who does family law."

Ana took a deep, calming breath. The whole conversation had her by the throat, and she still wasn't sure why talking about the legalities of their future made her nervous.

"Gah, that sounds big." She gulped. "We've been together for a bit over a year and we're already talking about a family lawyer."

She stared out of the window for a stretch of road, eyes glassy on the passing landscape. Sparse trees among medium-height buildings were barely more than green and light moving spots.

Liam continued to tap his fingers on the wheel. "What do you think about marriage? As an institution, I mean."

Ana closed her eyes again, her stomach rolling into itself.

She pushed her nerves down and shrugged. "I don't see the point of it to be honest. I didn't grow up dreaming about it and I don't think I've spent more than five seconds thinking of a wedding day. What is it for, nowadays? People get married, some stay together forever, some break up. I don't think it means much."

He scoffed but there was humor in it. "I guess I've known for a while that I didn't fall for you because of your romantic nature."

She chuckled. "I know. And I promise you, every time I make a comment like that around my parents, they say I'm causing all their gray hairs. But, remember my documentary, *Love in Times of Contempt*? I bet you would have thought me a romantic from that film."

"I remember. It was all about how it's worth looking for love because when it works, it's magical, right?"

"Yeah. I think love can be magical, but a wedding isn't necessary for it. If chances are people are going to break up anyway, why spend a year planning an expensive party?"

He laughed. "God, Ana. What about the celebration? Sure, marriage isn't what it used to be— and in many ways that's a good thing. I don't care for it being an economic arrangement— though that's still an aspect of it for many people. For insurance or whatever— or about social standing. I'd like to get married, though. I thought about it, once in a while, over the past few years. You know, in general terms."

"You did?" She tried to hide the fact that her hands shook by putting them under her thighs. She stared out of the windshield once more, gazing at the hills approaching near. She hoped Liam planned to stop for gas soon; she needed a chance to gather her wits and collect herself. Only then she might be able to understand her reaction to the conversation.

"Yeah. I see it as making a commitment that my wife and I are going to work at staying together. I want that kind of relationship in my life, as you know."

"I know."

Hills rose around them as they exited Los Angeles, dirt yellow-brown with trees and bushes giving it life, but she didn't see any details. She was talking about marriage with her boyfriend, an undercurrent of anxiety electrifying the layer right beneath her skin. She couldn't make sense of it, except for the voice in her mind telling her that marriage... that weddings...

"We're almost to the gas station," he said. "The same from our first car ride together. Remember?"

Lost in her thoughts, she didn't reply. She needed to stretch her legs and clear her head, because it sounded like... it seemed like...

"But, Liam," she said as if they were still in the middle of their conversation. Her voice came out louder, shock fueling her vocal cords. "If we want to be together 'til we're old, and you want to be a married man... does that mean...?"

He nodded, taking his eyes away from the road for a second. "I'd like to propose to you one day."

Ana lay back on her seat, eyes lost out of her window. The road signs passed them by fast, the posts of the road fences blurry.

She really, really needed to get stale coffee from the convenience store and let the bad taste distract her. She needed time to figure out what the hell her reaction was about.

She heard the blinkers again, and Liam drove the car into the gas station. He parked it next to a pump.

"What if it doesn't work that way?" she asked, her heart beating fast. As much as she wanted her voice to sound teasing, she heard the small tinge of panic in it. "Maybe we talk to the lawyer and decide it doesn't make sense to get married or... or I could propose to you."

He chuckled, reaching for his ball cap in the glove compartment. "We both know I'm the romantic one in this relationship. I wouldn't be opposed to you proposing as a grand gesture, but I think I will be the one actually planning something cheesy for us to remember."

She watched him put his cap on, and lean back to unlock his door. She stopped him from getting out of the vehicle with a hand on his thigh.

"We've talked about money and marriage," she said. "Should we talk about children? Do you want children in the future?"

He turned to her, surprised. "Uhm... yeah, I'd like children in the future. You?"

This she knew. "I think so, yeah, but not for a few more years."

He nodded again, reached across the car to kiss her. "It's decided, then. We're still very much compatible. We don't need to decide on the wedding stuff today."

He got out of the car and began filling up the tank; Ana stayed in the car for a minute, trying to compose herself.

"Right on time to meet your parents," she commented in a sotto voice as she made her way to the convenience store.

—

Liam parked the car at his parents' driveway. Every time he'd tried to make his schedule fit a visit to his parents with Ana, their plans had been thwarted by one thing or another; he'd been wanting this moment for a long time. He turned the engine off and took a deep breath, a grin about to burst on his face.

"Ready?" He placed a hand on her thigh.

"Eh… kinda." The slant on the line of her mouth told him enough, but he let her continue. "I hate to admit this but, now that we're here, I'm a teensy bit nervous."

He arched an eyebrow to hide the humor probably showing on his lips. She was kind of cute. "Really?"

"Really, what? Really, do I hate to admit it, or really, am I nervous? Because it's both."

"Why?" He let his smile take over. "They're so excited to meet you."

"Maybe it's the latina in me, with all the things my parents told me about respecting your elders and such, but I want to impress your mom and dad. Their opinion matters to you, right? I want it to be good."

"It will be." He squeezed the flesh of her quad, soft under his hand. "Remember how I was nervous about meeting your parents?"

"Yeah, but I knew how much they were going to love you, considering how hard they wanted me to date someone. And it went just like I told you— they loved you, they fed you, they didn't want to let you go. Even if you weren't super famous, they would have been starstruck."

Liam chuckled. "Oh, c'mon. They were happy you were with someone and that you were happy."

She lifted a hand for a quick caress on his stubbled cheek. "True. Is it gonna be the same with your parents?"

He leaned into her hand. "I think they'll be happy that I am happy."

She smiled. "Will they interrogate me the way my parents did to you?"

"You said it yourself, they wanted to get to know me in the way they do with everyone. And I don't think my parents will do the same."

She sighed and, with her free hand, reached for his on her thigh. Her palm rested warm on his skin. "Thanks, that helps."

She leaned across the car and kissed him. His heart turned into cotton fluff, the small moment reminding him, once again, that he was the luckiest guy on earth.

"Okay," she said. "I'm ready."

They got out of the car. He rushed to the trunk to get their bags, before leading Ana to his parents' door.

Giddiness filled every cubic inch of him, fueling the smile almost splitting his face in half. He didn't try to subdue it now; he'd talked to his family about Ana often, and it excited him that they would finally get to meet each other.

The double doors to his parents' house opened, and both his mom and dad were there, smiling.

"Oh, it's so nice to see you!" His mom hugged him tight, the warmth of it reaching to his soul. His dad followed.

Liam put a hand on Ana's lower back. "Mom, Dad, this is Ana."

"Hello," Ana said and, if he was not mistaken, she giggled when his mom pulled her in for a brief hug.

"Hello, Ana, it's lovely to meet you. Finally! I'm Julia. This," she said pointing at his dad, "is Steve."

"Come on in." Liam's dad shook Ana's hand and invited them in. He dropped a couple of slaps on Liam's back. "Welcome home, son."

Liam exchanged a smile with his dad, noting the older man's eyes shining with pride.

"We'll show you the rest of the house in a minute," his mom said, guiding Ana up the stairs. "We'll leave your things in your room first."

Ana glanced around his childhood home, with its staircase tucked to the side, and a living room, dining table, and kitchen island bar in a big open space. She followed his mom up the stairs, studying the mix of photos and paintings covering the wall next to them.

"I'm going to want to look at each one of them," Ana told Liam over her shoulder.

"You'll stay here," his mom continued. "It's Liam's old bedroom. When he gifted us the reno, we changed it a little to be more of a guest room."

Liam left his and Ana's bag on the bed in his old room. After giving Ana a quick rundown of the house, they settled in the kitchen where his mom and dad finished cooking dinner. Ana sat next to Liam at the kitchen island. He placed a hand on her thigh— patted it twice.

His dad offered to make them drinks while his mom puttered in the kitchen.

"Can I help you with anything?" Ana offered.

"Oh, no, not tonight, please." His mom dismissed the comment with a wave of her hand.

Liam leaned close to Ana, and spoke in a lower volume that did nothing to hide his words. "Don't insist. I know that tone of my mom's. It's her polite firm tone."

His mom smirked. "I agree. Listen to him on this one, Ana."

"Okay." Ana smiled. "I will, this time."

Liam squeezed the flesh of her thigh.

"Liam told us you two met through work?" Dad asked.

"Yes." Ana nodded. "We worked close together for a month or so last year for one of my documentaries and, well... things sparked from there."

"Right, yes, he'd mentioned that." Dad gave them their drinks, and moved the chopping board to the island to prepare a salad. "The documentary is coming out soon, correct?"

"In a month, more or less," Liam said. "Ana has refused to show me the final cut, so I guess it'll be a surprise for all of us."

Ana shook her head at him. "I told you I want you to have the full impact when we see it at the festival. And you've seen like 98% of it already, anyway."

"When are you going to that festival again?" His mom asked. She washed yellow peppers and, cutting the tops off, gave them to his dad to chop and add to the salad. It seemed like a simple gesture, but it told Liam how in sync his parents still were. It made him hope the same for him and Ana; a future where they wouldn't need to talk to stay coordinated. Where they knew each other so deeply that they moved as one.

A smile curled his lips. He believed they'd get there, sooner rather than later. Liam leaned to the side and kissed Ana on the temple.

"We're flying to Canada in a few weeks," she replied through a smile. "We're booked for several interviews and meetings. The premiere is on our third night there." She sighed. "I'm still in shock that we're going to be premiering in Toronto!"

Ana reached for his hand on her leg, and he interlocked their fingers together.

"I still think changing agents was the right thing for both of us," Ana continued, gazing at Liam. "Jen is awesome with you and mine, Reagan, is great too... but I have to admit, Coulton did set me up for great things, when he offered me that job with you. It would have taken me a long time or creating an outstanding film to get to Toronto before all this happened."

Liam frowned. "Coulton had an idea, but it wasn't out of generosity. He wanted to keep me working, and you were the right solution at the time."

"That's true. And it was Jen and Reagan who managed to get us at the Toronto Festival—"

"And your own great work," Liam interrupted, squeezing her hand and grinned at her.

She gave him one of her glorious smiles and leaned in to kiss him, right as a knock at the door caught everyone's attention.

"That must be Alex," his dad said.

Liam hated the way his stomach dropped, taking away the glow of the moment.

Chapter Five

ANA'S NERVES CALMED DOWN once she started chatting with Liam's parents. She studied them as they cooked, fascinated by the traces of Liam she found in them. Liam had his dad's height and general shape, and his mom's eyes and smile. They also seemed to prefer casual conversation, rather than the questions her parents shot at Liam when she took him to meet them.

Liam had been his supportive self, sparking gratitude and the appearance of a grin on her face. The knock on the door interrupted the moment. Alex's arrival seemed to cause the shuttering of Liam's eyes, his energy hiding away inside of him somewhere.

Tension appeared on Liam's lips. Memories of little things he'd shared with her about Alex came back and, as curious as she was to meet her boyfriend's brother, her loyalties were clear. If conflict broke out between them, Ana would step to Liam's side.

Steve opened the door and, after a brief hug between them, Alex made his way into the kitchen.

Liam had told her they looked relatively similar and she could see it. They were about the same height, although Alex's form was of long muscles, rather than developed like Liam's. His hair shone at a darker shade and, as he came closer and stood in front of Liam and her, she could see his eyes were hazel, rather than the bright green of Liam's eyes.

Alex stared at Ana and, if her gut was right, that was at least in part because he meant to ignore Liam. Ana stole a glance at her boyfriend, gauging the situation; he had a slight frown but seemed expectant more than anything.

Ana turned back to Alex and gave him a friendly wave.

"Hi, Alex. I'm Ana," she said.

Alex put his hands in his pockets and nodded. "Hello, Ana." To her surprise, his voice carried a deeper bass than Liam's. He watched her intensely. "I don't think I've met one of Liam's girlfriends since college. I've seen some in magazine covers at the grocery store till before, of course, but I think you're the first one he's brought home."

Ana squinted at him, assessing the best response to the indirect, subtle dig. Undecided, she glanced at Liam, who stared at Alex with the same expression as before, and Julia, whose eyes jumped between her sons.

Ana turned back to Alex, her gaze on him steady. "I'm glad all of our schedules finally aligned. Liam talks about his family often; I'm happy to be meeting you all."

"Yeah, we finally made it happen," Liam said next to her. There was a degree of hardness in his voice.

Alex stood still except for his eyes, which shifted to Liam. "Hello. It's been a while."

"How are you?" Liam asked.

Air hung heavily around them. Ana checked with Julia again; they locked eyes briefly.

"Fine." Alex turned and walked away, turning around the island in silent dismissal of Liam and giving his mom a hug. "Hi, mom."

Ana tracked him across the kitchen, with a confusing mix of uncertainty and irritation lodging in her stomach. She was pretty sure Julia whispered something in Alex' ear, but she didn't hear what it was.

"Okay, I will," Alex replied, grumbly and low. "How's work, brother dear?"

His voice had turned brighter, louder, and fake.

Julia frowned and shook her head. "Please, Alex." She turned to Ana. "I'm so sorry. These two have always known how to push each other's buttons. We were never able to get them out of the habit."

"I'd like to point out I've pushed no buttons," Liam said to Ana's side, his hand reaching to her waist and pulling her close. She surrounded his waist with her arm, squeezing in what she hoped was a comforting manner.

Alex' eyes followed the gesture. His face remained immobile, except for the slightest change to the tension on his lips.

"Except for that one comment, you mean." Julia arched an eyebrow.

Ana glanced at Liam, who smirked. "Except for that one, Mom."

"Anyway, do you want a drink, Alex?" Steve offered. "Dinner's almost ready."

Ana and Liam sat at the kitchen island again, but Alex remained away. He leaned against the counter where his mom worked.

Ana changed the subject. Maybe it would lift the spirit of the room. "I noticed some of the paintings here look a lot like the ones in your house, Liam." A whisper of a thought questioned whether she should have said *our house*, but she squashed it for later contemplation. "Are they from the same artist?"

"It's two different artists," Liam replied. "Mom and Alex."

"What?! And you never told me?" Ana blanched.

He chuckled. "I... guess I didn't, sorry. I thought you'd have noticed the signatures."

"They're beautiful." Ana gazed at Liam's mom, who had a soft smile on her face. Alex's face, on the other hand, was hard as a stone. Ana whipped her eyes back to Julia. "I always thought they looked like the works of two different people; I guess I was right. Are yours the more abstract ones or the other style?"

"Mine are the abstract ones—" she started to say, but Alex interrupted her.

"You have some of my stuff up in your place?" His voice was deep and aggravated.

Ana barely noticed that she was looking back and forth between the brothers, just like their mom had before.

"Yeah." Liam responded with a hint of a challenge in his tone. Ana knew him well enough to know he regretted it; he tried to do better and added, "of course."

Alex frown deepened. "You should take them down."

"What? No. I like them."

"They really are great," Ana tried.

"Maybe you could come see them." Liam put his arm around her again, pulling her to him. "They really do look good. And we'd love to have you there."

Alex shook his head. "Maybe. One day."

"Alex," his dad admonished.

"I didn't ask him to buy those." Alex scowled and looked out of the window.

"That's not what this is about." Liam's hand pressed against Ana's skin, and she put a hand over his, sending him as much comfort as she could.

"He was trying to support you," Steve said at the same time.

Julia sighed. "I hope you prepared poor Ana for this, Liam."

Julia's concern broke the spell.

Liam had turned to check on Ana, and she watched his face transform from sudden worry to relief. "I didn't. Not quite for this."

"It doesn't scare me." Ana gave Liam a peck. She couldn't help it; she smiled. "I can take two brothers quarreling."

Liam kissed her temple.

"And with that," Julia said as she opened the oven, "dinner is ready."

Ana tip-toed into the guest room, hoping to avoid disrupting the conversation she'd stumbled upon. She didn't want Alex and his mom to hear her and realize she'd accidentally eavesdropped on them. She closed the door behind her with a soft click, and focused on Liam standing at the other side of the bed. She'd caught him changing clothes, his shirt falling down his torso and covering his defined abs. She'd already changed; she got in bed, burrowing under the comforter. Liam followed.

They faced each other and he pulled her close. He sighed deeply, relief softening his body into the mattress. She ran her fingers over the side of his face.

"How are you doing?" she asked. The worried wrinkles on his forehead relaxed.

"Better now." His eyes, closed up to that point, opened to fasten with hers, the green of his irises mossy.

"Dinner was... a bit tense." She smirked.

Liam scoffed. "I appreciate how you and my parents tried to make it feel normal."

"How long has this been going on with Alex? I just heard your mom chastising him for his behavior at dinner, but she seemed concerned, too."

"What do you mean, you heard Mom do that?"

"I was coming out of the bathroom and I dropped my hair tie." Ana wiggled her wrist in front of him, showing him her usual spot for it. "I may have moved very slowly to retrieve it, when I realized whose voices I could hear from the first floor. I didn't hear much, though."

Liam chuckled, but the humor didn't overtake his general look of frustration over everything Alex-related. "What did you hear?"

"Your mom was saying that she wanted him to make more of an effort. He first said that he didn't feel the need to, but then she pressed him and he admitted he didn't have it in him. That seemed to worry her."

The door of the room next to Ana and Liam closed; the sound reached them even though it hadn't seemed like a particularly forceful action. Alex had gotten into his room.

Liam's voice turned low, only for Ana's ears. "I don't know what's happening with him. He doesn't talk to me, but my mom has told me a bit. I'm missing details, but I think he hates his job, which may or may not be related to why he doesn't paint anymore, and he hates all of it."

"So he takes it out on you?" Ana frowned. "He's so dry and short with you."

Liam lifted his free shoulder in a half-shrug. "I've been dry and cynical with him, too. I suspect he doesn't believe yet that I've changed, that I'm trying to be different; we haven't spent enough time together, either, for him to see it for himself. And, not gonna lie, he does irk me— and it shows. You saw me."

She nodded and let her hand travel to his shoulder, where she massaged the tense flesh underneath.

"My mom asked me to check in with you that you do feel okay," he added. "I think she was irritated at Alex that he couldn't be a bit kinder today; maybe even a bit embarrassed."

"Oh, don't worry about me. All families have these tensions. My dad's brother never spoke to him again after my parents decided to stay in the US. A little squabble between you and Alex doesn't bother me."

His hand found the skin of her lower back, fingers splaying.

"It does make me a bit sad, though," she continued, "because I know you want it to be different."

He gazed into her eyes, a soft smile on his lips. He kissed her softly. "I do."

"And I know you're trying. I can see it." She traced one of his eyebrows with the pad of her finger.

Liam's hand found its way beneath the fabric of her pajama shirt. "I had an idea earlier. It might be a bad one. Or an excellent one."

"Oh?"

"Alex has an MBA. Did I ever mention that? He's high up on a CFO-for-hire team."

"No, you didn't." She arched an eyebrow. "You should really tell me more about this kinda thing, you know?"

His eyes sparkled. "I've been too busy telling you that I love you. And about my day."

"I guess you have been." She chuckled. "Cheeky. But tell me more about this idea of yours. It involves Alex, I assume?"

"Yeah. As far as I know, his plan was to get to a well-paid position fast, one which would give him enough disposable time and income to paint. I'm not sure what happened, but he's been stuck for a while."

"I think I know where this is going..."

He scrunched up his face. "What would you think if we offered him the Manager of Operations position?"

"Yep. I saw that coming." She squinted at him. "Tell me more."

"It's something Linda said, asking me to think about what I'd be willing to do to help Alex. Did you see him during dinner? When he wasn't restless, he looked so..."

"Vacant."

Liam sighed. "Yeah. That fits."

"So you want to hire him... to help him." She frowned. "Sounds like the production company may yet be a family business, then."

"I get it if you have concerns. I would have them, too— I do. So let's interview him like we did Ely. And I hope you know... I wouldn't do this if I didn't think he's good. This just happens to kill two birds with one stone. I can't do much about his painting but this... I can help him a bit with the job situation. If you're okay with it."

"It's kind of... daring, wouldn't you say? He may be good with business things, but if he's going to fight you all the time..."

"Maybe. I just had this image in my head, let's say, or hope— that if we worked together and spent more time together, we'd have a chance to get a bit closer."

She shook her head with a hesitant smile escaping her. "You know that if you tell me like that, I'm more likely to want to say yes, don't you? Just to support you."

He grinned, unapologetic. "Yeah."

She chuckled and shook her head. "Let's talk to him and see. Good thing I'm a latina and we do this kind of thing for family all the time."

He pushed her to her back and climbed on top of her. "You're my favorite latina."

"Oomph, get off," she said. "You're too heavy! I can't breathe."

He laughed and turned them again, this time bringing her to rest on top of him, the blankets messy and half-off them.

"It's all of the muscle mass," he explained, unnecessarily. His hands traveled from her waist and lower back to her ass, where he grabbed two handfuls.

She rolled her eyes. "Of course. We don't want to forget your physique is well built."

"It's for work." His smile was impish.

"So you've said in the past." She tried to hide her smile, but suspected she was unsuccessful. She ignored the way he squeezed her flesh. "You've also said you liked being looked at for it."

His eyes shone with playfulness. "No, I said I like that you like it."

"That was before I realized how hard it feels." She arched an eyebrow and used her index finger to poke on a hard pectoral muscle. "Like granite. No give. Not very cuddly, you know?"

His laugh filled the room, the rumble of it reverberating under her.

"Ssshh," she exclaimed. "Remember Alex is in the room next door."

"I just finished filming; I haven't had the chance to fully rehydrate myself. Eat yummy treats again."

His grin didn't dim. It lit up her heart.

She kissed his temple, his high cheekbones, the curve of his jaw. "We sure should make the most out of the time we have until your next project. Feed you properly."

His hands came up to run his fingers through her hair and fan it around her face. He sighed again, but this time it held a note of pleasure, rather than exhaustion.

"I love you, Ana Lira."

"I love you too, Liam McMillan."

He cradled her face, guiding her down to his lips. He kissed her with reverence; melting into the moment was easy. Pressing her pelvis against his hardening cock even more so.

"Can you keep quiet?" His pupils dilated, eyelids growing heavy.

"Not if you do your job right."

His fingers dug into her skull, and he pushed his knee between her legs to encourage them open. "Is that a dare?"

She sat up on him, straddling his hips, hands on his chest. The blankets still on her slid off her back with a soft caress. "Of course not. We really need to be quiet."

He lifted his torso and kissed her neck, taking off her shirt. "Good, because I happen to know how loud you can get."

She ground her hips against him and freed him from his shirt, too. "That's why I'll be doing the work."

"Is that right?"

He pushed her back onto the bed and kicked the comforter and sheets away from over them; they both did quick work of getting rid of the remaining clothes.

She pounced on him. She placed a hand on his shoulder to keep him laying flat on the bed; she kissed a nipple and nibbled on the taut skin of his belly. His hand curved around her nape, holding on to her, suggesting.

He didn't need to ask. She grabbed his hard cock with a hand and wrapped her lips around the head, sucking. The tremor that traveled under his skin blew oxygen into her own desire.

"Yes," he panted, his free hand pillowing his head high to watch her. "More."

She took him into her mouth. He grabbed her hair into a fist, guiding her speed and angle. She let him use her lips and tongue on himself, and grabbed his shaft with a firm hand. She used her own saliva as lubrication, twisting her hand in sync with her mouth. Her body asked for more, warmth and desire pooling inside of her, fueled by his hard breathing and barely hidden whimpers.

Her craving of him intensified, but she wouldn't give in to it yet. Not until she sensed him at the brink. She held onto the power of it; how she pushed him further along to the edge.

Soon. She moaned. He made a strangled sound. So soon.

She sucked him hard, tongue rubbing that point on the underside that drove him wild, and released him.

He surprised her by guiding her head away from his cock and bringing her up for a deep kiss.

"Ride me," he said. "I want to come inside of you."

"So demanding for someone not in control."

She settled on top of him again, grabbing him with a hand and slowly sinking down on him. Another moan escaped her as he filled her.

His hand grabbed the flesh of her hips. "Sshh. These walls weren't part of the reno. They for sure are not soundproof."

She bit her lip and started moving on him, building up the pace. "Don't talk about a reno while I'm on top of you, Liam."

He chuckled but the sound devolved into a whimper. "God. Ana."

One of his hands grabbed a bouncing breast, while the other found the right angle to rub on her clit. Her legs burned but she kept at it, angling her hips to get his cock to hit the right spot inside of her, almost sobbing at the stimulation of him and his two fingers.

"Are you gonna come on my cock yet?" he asked.

"Shh." Her legs couldn't keep at it and she shifted her movement, rolling her hips back and forth. "Rub me harder."

He added a third finger and gave her a feral smile, his other hand playing with her nipple. She pushed the hand away and dropped her torso to him, a choked sob escaping her despite her best intentions. His free hand kneaded her ass and thick thighs as she licked his bottom lip, nibbled on it, and pulled at it with her teeth.

Her hands squeezed the hard curves of his shoulders and, lifting her torso again, she surrounded his strong neck with her hands. She felt his gulp against them.

"I like knowing I hold power over you." She arched her back, teasing them both with almost disconnection, before taking him deep into her again. "That you're strong and could dominate me, but let me take you."

"I love that you want to." His voice rasped out of him, his eyes tracking her body as if taking in every single detail.

Her legs trembled with the effort, and she let herself squeeze his neck a touch harder. "I want to. So badly."

"I can see the strain. Let me help." He wet his bottom lip in a slow swipe of his tongue.

Her muscles and tendons numb, her clit cried for friction. He grabbed her hips with firm hands again, fingers digging into her plump flesh, keeping them in place as he braced his feet on the bed.

"Say yes. Let me do this." His eyes roamed her face, watchful. "You know I can do this. I'll give you what you need."

She let go of his neck, hands on his shoulders again, and she dug her nails into him.

"Show me."

No sooner than the words had left her, he pushed his hips up and drove into her.

"Yes. Hell," she panted.

He doubled his speed. "I knew you'd break. I love doing this to you."

"Fuck. Liam." It was her turn to whimper. "Right there. Oh my god. This position is too good."

She must have gotten louder, because he admonished her.

"Shhhh, quiet." Her voice died in her throat, unconsciously doing as he said.

Despite his body working hard to fuck her, and although his voice sounded raspy, he didn't seem breathless. She, on the other hand, couldn't keep up. Her body melted, taking his fervent attack in. He wrapped his arms around her, holding on to her as he pumped hard into her, her mind blank, not enough air in her lungs.

"That's right," he said. "Good girl."

Her orgasm exploded without warning, tremors waving and cresting through her body. She shook against him, his arms tightening up around her.

"F—fuck," he said, keeping up the frenzied rhythm of his hips. "There's— nothing— better... God. Nothing better— than you coming— on my cock."

The haze of her climax dissipated, her senses catching on to the room again: the muffled sounds of their breathing and straining bed frame, the clean smell of their sweat, the dim light of a bed lamp.

The grin she gave him felt feline on her face.

"I can take you. Fuck me 'til you come."

"Holy shit. Keep talking like that."

She raked her nail over his chest, relishing on his glazed eyes and slack mouth. "You want me to tell you how good you feel?"

"Yeah."

"How I feel tender and raw and I love what you do to me?"

"Fuck. Yes."

"That the way you fill me up makes me feel on fire?"

"Ana—"

His hips buckled and faltered as he spilled himself into her.

"Yes, like that," she said, bending down to kiss his jaw.

Still connected, she rested on top of him, head on his shoulder. She could smell the faint traces of cologne and sweat on his neck, sweet and musk and intoxicating.

His arms had loosened up around her as he recovered, but tightened again in a loving hold around her back.

"I sometimes don't have the words to describe how perfectly you fit me," he said. "I wish I did."

She kissed his clavicle and moved to his side, gentle in their decoupling.

"I don't need poetry." She watched him turn to his side again, putting them right back to the same position in which their evening had begun. "As long as you love me."

He sighed. "That I do."

"We managed to keep quiet, right?"

"I think so. If not, it's just Alex."

"Just Alex?" She chuckled. "Something tells me he'd happily say something crude to your parents about it, if he heard us."

He grinned. "So? We're adults."

"Ew. That's all."

He laughed. "C'mere."

He straightened the arm closest to the mattress out, offering her his shoulder. She scooted forward, happy for the cuddle. With his free arm, he turned off the side lamp.

With slowing, whispered words, they went to sleep in each other's arms.

Chapter Six

AFTER TAKING TURNS IN the shower and getting ready for the day— Liam had almost jumped Ana when she came into the room smelling all fresh, the scent of her shampoo filling the space, but she'd deterred him— Ana and Liam joined the family for brunch.

"I hope you slept well," Dad said as he and Mom moved around the kitchen. Liam approached Mom and kissed her cheek.

"We did," Ana replied from nearby. "Can I help with cutting up fruit?"

She settled by the island to help while Liam made sure everyone had coffee. He focused on setting up the table next, keeping up with the easy conversation around him.

He took a break to sip from his mug. "I know my room looks different and it's not the same bed, but sleeping at home hits different. We almost slept in."

Alex came into the kitchen, a half-frown already in place. "Might have had to do with staying up. You two made noise until late. I heard laughing across the wall."

Liam tried to stop the automatic clenching of his jaw at the sight of his brother, and arched an eyebrow instead. "That's all you heard, though, right?"

Ana turned to Liam with eyes open wide. It brought humor back into him; he held back the rueful smile it provoked and hid it behind a smirk. Alex, on the other hand, stared back at Liam with derision.

"What?" Liam put as much innocence in his voice as he could. His parents were doing their best to ignore them, but he didn't want to push it. "She snores loudly sometimes, but I'm used to it."

"Shush," Ana rolled her eyes and returned to her task.

Alex arched an eyebrow and turned away, dismissing Liam with a scowl and getting coffee for himself.

"Breakfast is ready," his mom said. "Let's eat."

They all sat around the kitchen nook to share the meal. The sound of clinking cutlery and the smell of warm food enveloped Liam, and he dug into it with complete abandon.

"So how are things progressing with the production company?" His mom asked.

"We hired someone," Liam replied. "Her name is Ely. She's Ana's best friend and has been in the not-for-profit area for a long time. She'll be in charge of the Social Impact department and I think it'll be a great fit."

"You obviously don't have problems working with people you're close to," his dad said. "Since you're in a relationship and have this company together."

"I actually think that it can be a great thing." Ana buttered a warm bun as she added her thoughts. "So many businesses talk about being a family but it's just... propaganda, if you will. Working with people you're close to— as long as you share the same passion— it makes it real, to think of a company like a team."

"But people still have to have what it takes to do the job." Alex took a sip of his coffee. He hadn't touched the food yet. "If your friend doesn't know what she's doing, passion and friendship won't help."

Liam swallowed a bite and ground his teeth together. "Agreed. That's why we're doing our best not to be impulsive. Ely is wonderful as a person and when we chatted about the position, she had all the right answers. Her resume backed it up, too."

"She'll have to change her mindset if she's coming in from the not-for-profit world." Alex finally reached for some fruit, and added several pieces to his plate. He did not give Liam his eyes. "She'll have to adjust in a company like yours. People from NFPs think about things differently than for profits and there's a sort of cultural shock in changing worlds."

"Ely told us that it's not the case so much anymore," Ana said, "as many NFP organizations are trying to follow a profit model, to make the best use of resources."

"That's true, but she'll likely need strong guidelines to not overburden the rest of the company." Alex speared a slice of orange and lifted hard eyes at Ana. "You'll have to define what's a healthy dynamic between socially-centered departments and operational departments."

"Do you have any suggestions?" Liam asked, briefly locking eyes with Ana. She gave him a slight nod. She agreed they could go ahead with a first casual interview.

Alex shrugged. His eyes returned to his plate. "I'm sure you know, typically, the expectation is you'll allocate a percentage of earnings towards funding the social initiatives. Whatever your social focus, it should be broken down into different specific budgets, maybe even have the social impact department test or prove where they're putting the investments... or even have it apply for it, in some sort of grants setups."

Ana drank some of her coffee, a small groove between her eyebrows. "I don't like the idea of setting up the social department to fight for money. The way Liam and I, the consultants, and the lawyers discussed it, there'll be a base budget and a floating budget dependent on profit. But we could potentially use some sort of grant application system somewhere, to let the youth apply for it as part of their learning experience."

Alex gazed at Ana, seeming to be okay having a conversation with her if not with Liam. "Mom told me you had a lawyer doing all the paperwork and setting up a big chunk of the company and processes, right?"

"Yeah." Liam tracked Alex's response to his words. "We have some drafts for how all of this would work, but Ana and I agreed we wanted to see what the managers suggested for their departments."

Liam added his two cents, and it didn't surprise him that Alex continued to watch Ana instead of acknowledging him. Liam ground his teeth.

"It all sounds amazing," His dad said. "Well thought out."

"Our plan is to hold meetings with both Ely and the Manager of Operations to define the structure in detail," Liam added. He gazed at Ana for a second, relieved when she stared back at him and nodded, giving him permission to move ahead. He took a deep breath before continuing. "Do you want to be there?"

Liam studied Alex's reaction once more, steeling his back when his brother whipped his head to glare at Liam.

"You're talking to me?"

Liam nodded, nostrils flaring.

"Why would I want to be in those meetings?" Alex placed both hands on each side of his plate.

Ana put her hand over Liam's. It was only then that he realized he'd curled it into a fist. "We were wondering if you might be interested in the Manager of Operations position."

His mom gasped. "You're offering him a job at the production company?"

"That's great, Alex! Liam!" his dad added.

Ana squeezed Liam's hand.

"You're offering me a position in your company?" Alex asked, lacking the joy everyone else's voice held. "In LA?"

"Yes," Ana said. "You shared good ideas, and Liam told me about your degrees and current job. If you think your experience fits the role and has transferable skills, then we'd like to start holding meetings to structure things and get it all going."

"My experience would fit the role, especially if I'm helping set it up." Alex frowned, a small scowl on his lips. "What I'm not sure of is whether LA fits me. If a company like this is what I want. If working for Liam is what I want."

Liam interlocked his fingers with Ana's and stared at her, pleading telepathically for her to take the lead. He didn't trust himself to not get snarky with Alex. She seemed to understand.

"We plan to start with the meetings in a month or so." With her free hand, Ana took a sip of water, holding Alex's attention. "My friend is moving to LA in three weeks, giving us a week to settle in before we start with the final company set up. After that, Liam and I are flying to Toronto for the festival, and during that week, the managers are to meet to prep for the meetings we want to have after we come back to LA."

Alex turned away and stared out the window, all four pairs of eyes watching him.

Alex crossed his arms, his eyes still fixed outside. "So you're telling me you'd like an answer from me by then, am I getting that right?"

"You are," Liam said.

Chapter Seven

THE NEXT EVENING, ANA followed Liam into a local sushi restaurant. He held her hand and guided her into the building, accompanied by Logan and his fiancée, Giuliana. Liam and Logan had eaten here before; they'd discovered the place while they were roommates in undergrad, and had never stopped coming whenever Liam visited home. They liked it because the food was excellent and it had small-group rooms separate from the main dining space. It gave them the privacy they needed to enjoy their meal together without much interruption.

The four of them sat on the elegant wooden Zaisu around a low table.

Logan grinned, all charm. "It's nice finally meeting you face to face."

Ana smiled. She had chatted with him briefly over the phone the past year, when he and Liam had been on a call. The small cell phone screen hadn't done him justice. His dark brown skin was smooth and flawless; his hair coiled in a tight curl, which he styled in twists and a sharp fade. Next to him, Giuliana's eyes shone. Her curls were wide and her skin had the deep tan of

Mediterranean ancestry. Sitting side by side, they fit well, two fashionable people on a double date with friends.

"I'm so glad we get to do this," Ana said.

They ordered and settled into an easy conversation. A little while later, their server arrived and they all picked food onto their plates.

"How long ago did you two get together?" Giuliana asked.

"Over a year ago." Ana reached for Liam's hand on his lap. "How long ago was the engagement?"

She remembered it happening: Logan had called to give Liam the news, a few months into the relationship. They had been talking more often, and Ana's heart had warmed with Liam's joy that Logan thought to call him the next day.

"Eight months," Logan said. Him and Giuliana shared a long, soft, adoring look.

"The invitations were gorgeous." Ana mixed soy sauce and wasabi in a small round dish. "We both made sure to book the date off from our schedules. It's coming up fast!"

Liam added ginger and wasabi to one of his rolls. "Mo told me that he heard from my tailor. My suit is getting made to the specs you sent, so I'll be ready on time, too."

Giuliana sighed. "Thanks. Good to know at least that is going well. People talk about how much work there is in organizing a wedding but, wow, is it a lot. If you two ever plan a wedding, definitely hire a planner."

Ana put down the roll she'd picked up and drank some water instead.

"Giuls, c'mon." Logan elbowed his fiancée. "It's been just a year for them."

Coarse rope tied itself around Ana's ribcage. It *had* been just a year.

"What?" Giuliana argued. "I didn't say with each other. I just put it out there that they might plan a wedding one day and to get professional help if that's the case."

"How is that better?" Logan shook his head.

Liam laughed. Ana tried to smile, but her facial muscles tightened instead. The idea of marriage settled in her stomach like lead... and she hated it.

"I might want to elope," Ana blurted. "If I ever— or we— you know."

She sensed Liam's eyes on her, but Ana focused on Logan.

"We tried to keep it small," he said, "but Giuliana's family didn't let us. Families can get messy, man. They all have an opinion on what a wedding should look like."

"I'm sure my family would be okay with keeping it small, thankfully." Liam turned to Ana. "Do you think your family would?"

She gulped. She glanced at him but talked to the group at large. "I think so. My parents don't know what to make of me, because I'm not a lawyer or a doctor and I was single for so long. They drop comments all the time about how they don't actually expect me to get married because, according to them, I'm too different and young people in America don't like to get married. They kind of throw their hands up in the air a bit. And the rest of my family is all in Ecuador so, really, I can do whatever I want. If I ever wanted to plan a wedding, I don't think I'd need to do more than let my parents call a few people."

Green lasers tracked the side of her head as Ana dipped a roll into soy sauce. Their server checked in on them, giving her a reprieve from the conversation. Unconcerned, Giuliana told them about the many things they still had to do in preparation for their wedding.

Ana took a deep breath and went back to her food.

"How did you two meet?" She asked the couple.

"At a mutual friend's party." Giuliana picked up a piece of sashimi. "I was there to meet someone else for a casual first date, but met Logan instead and we connected right away."

"If that guy had been there," Logan added, "she might have not given me the time of day. It's a scary thought."

Giuliana grinned. "I don't know about that. I noticed you right away so, if the guy had been there but had been a douche, I might've still ditched him for you."

One of Logan's eyebrows arched high as he looked at her, amused. "Ruthless— but I'm glad to hear it."

She gave him a sly smile, before turning back to Ana and Liam. "You two met at work, I believe?"

Ana added more wasabi to her plate. "Yes, though such a statement kinda hides the uniqueness of it."

"It was for the documentary, right?" Logan said. "Ana's the director."

"Director, editor, producer..." Liam kissed her temple. "She's amazing."

Ana's body relaxed completely at his words. She grinned at him.

"I can't wait to go watch it," Giuliana said.

"I'd love to hear what you think." Ana picked some ginger with her chopsticks. "We're a bit nervous about some scenes."

Giuliana frowned. "How come?"

"It focuses a lot on the rough side of fame: loneliness, fakeness, tabloids," Ana explained. "I was very careful during the editing process to make sure we didn't single out any culprits. We don't want to make it seem like Liam's angry at a particular person or group for what was happening in his career, but you never know."

Liam appeared to take a break from eating, placing a hand behind Ana's back. "I think some people in the industry could get angry at me— at us— for how the film shows its flaws."

"And, as we're setting up a production company, well... it could really make it tough for us to network."

"I see." Logan took a drink. "Hopefully people are not upset."

"Talking about the company, guess who we offered the Manager of Operations position to." Liam scratched an eyebrow as he watched his friend.

Logan's eyes shot back and forth between Liam and Ana. "Who?"

"Alex," Liam replied.

This time, both of Logan's eyebrows shot up. He let out a slow whistle. "I hope that works out, man."

Liam nodded. "Me too. It's a bit of a risk, but I know if he joins us he'll do a good job. He's prickly but I think he has integrity."

"And he's your brother." Ana placed a hand on his thigh and squeezed.

After wrapping up dinner and talking about some ideas for how they could meet in the future— going somewhere else together, the four of them, or having them in LA— they went out of the restaurant for a quick goodbye.

As Ana hugged Logan and Giuliana, she caught the first flash of a camera from the corner of her eye. She and Liam had been holding hands, as usual, and she squeezed his fingers in hers. Without words, they did their best to ignore whoever was taking shots of them and, getting back in their car, they drove around for a while before going back to Liam's parents' house.

Chapter Eight

A MONTH PASSED WITHOUT hearing from Alex.

After another family breakfast together the next day, Ana and Liam had driven back to LA. They followed the trip with a week's worth of meetings, and getting things up to date with her and Liam's agents and lawyers. By the next Sunday, Liam had flown out for a series of sponsorship TV ads and a photoshoot: watches, alcohol, and sports equipment.

On a tight schedule, within three weeks, Ana had broken her lease, donated her furniture, and packed the remainder of her things to ship back to LA. She got back to her new, official home two days before Ely was scheduled to land, and prepared to welcome her best friend into their new lives. Ana couldn't wait.

Taking Liam's SUV, still their only car, Ana drove to the airport with an unfaltering grin splitting her face. The hug Ana gave Ely when she came through the doors was of epic proportions, even though they had seen each other only two days before.

"I can't believe I'm officially living in LA." Ely settled on the passenger seat next to Ana. "It's exhilarating. I love change."

Ana started the car and began the journey home. Seeing her best friend with her in California filled Ana with butterflies, even as she shook her head at Ely's statement.

"Ay, Ely. Only you could say something like that." Ana took a left turn and got out of the parkade. "How long do we have to find you a place?"

"My parents should be here with the truck next Thursday and we're putting my stuff into storage, so I don't have to worry. It'll all be there until I find my place. Unless I've found a place, of course, but who knows."

"Your parents are awesome, to be driving your things all the way here."

"Yes they are, and they're very excited about it, actually. They're taking it as a road trip! They left last Saturday; they're following the scenic route. They expect to be here next Tuesday or Wednesday."

Ana overtook a slow car with ease. Soon they'd be stuck in traffic, so she delighted in the opportunity. "Where are they staying? They may have come up with excuses not to stay with us, but they have to at least accept an invitation for dinner."

"I don't remember the name of the hotel, but that's a good idea. Though you know my mom, she'll want to cook."

"C'mon. She'd be our guest. We can't make her cook."

Ely waved a hand in dismissal. "That's okay. My mom wouldn't know what to do with herself if she wasn't the one hosting the meal. I can get her to send me the shopping list for whatever dish she'd like to make, then we buy and prepare everything around it. Patacón *will* be involved, knowing her... which I'm sure will make you happy."

"Yes, ugh. I haven't had a good patacón in a long time. Probably since the last time your parents had me over. You think your mom will still want to make me some? Isn't she angry with me and renounced me as an adoptive daughter, now that I stole you away from them?"

"No, no." Ely laughed. "They said they've felt like empty nesters for long enough that they've already learned to make the most of it. You know, they said how I broke their hearts already five years ago when I moved out, et cetera. Me living in LA gives them a reason to travel around more, I think."

Ana grinned as she brought the car to a stop. They had reached the first bout of traffic. "Great, because I wouldn't want them to get into a feud with me."

Ely winked at Ana. "Don't worry, they won't. Talking about feuds, have you heard from Alex?"

"No." Ana scrunched up her nose. "We told him we needed his answer in about a month— that was a month ago. I told Liam last night, we should have given him a firm date. *About a month* gives him too much leeway and now we're a bit in limbo."

"So when you say you haven't heard from him, you mean nothing at all? Not only no definitive answer but not even a text or anything?" Ely reached for a water bottle in the console.

"That's right. Complete radio silence. Liam is irritated as hell, of course, but trying to be true to his word and give Alex time to think. Meanwhile, we did start a search for candidates, because we don't want to string our business along just because Alex doesn't want to commit. There's a couple of people who seem like they could be a good fit."

Ely gulped some water before continuing. "But if Alex says yes... then it'll be Alex?"

"Probably. On paper, he is a good fit. Liam showed me Alex's profile on his employer's website and it's actually quite impressive. It's the other stuff that worries me. When I met him, he was so... unapproachable. A bit antagonizing. At the same time, I don't want to push Liam too much. He did let me hire you."

"But I am good. On paper and otherwise."

Ana laughed. "We know that! Of course we do. At the end of the day, we wouldn't have hired you and wouldn't have offered the job to Alex if we had any doubts you could actually do the job. It's the personal stuff that makes it a bit muddy. Liam is trusting me and my love for you to think you'll be a great personable addition to the team."

Ely shrugged. "He knows me a bit, too."

"Sure, but it can get weird, right? Working with family. And you're as much my family as Alex is to Liam. So he's trusting me that I trust you."

"And you're trusting Liam with his choice of Alex. Thing is, having a family business is totally a normal thing. Not only for us latine people. The part that I don't get is that they don't like each other, and why Liam doesn't seem concerned about it."

The car inched slowly forward. Ana barely registered it as the ordeal it usually was... she had Ely, now.

Ana sighed. "They don't like each other and Liam *is* worried about it. Part of it is that Liam does know you and I think he hopes that with the three of us in it, Alex will soften and it'll make it easier for them to get that good relationship Liam wants."

Ana gazed at her friend, who'd frowned.

Ely nodded. "I'll do my best to aid in this crusade. I'm not going to disappoint you or Liam, I promise."

Ana winked and brought her eyes back to the car in front of them. "I know you won't."

———

Once they finally arrived at Ana and Liam's home, they put Ely's things away in the guestroom— the same room Ana had used when she first met Liam— and spent the evening talking on the patio and looking at listings. The next day, they spent the morning driving and talking whenever traffic was too slow, and Ana showed Ely around.

Liam was scheduled to arrive that evening, surely carrying many new freebies. In preparation to wait for him, Ana ordered lunch for herself and Ely, and they took the afternoon off to relax. They put on their bikinis and jumped into the swimming pool, lazily treading water.

"This is all just... amazing, Ana. Amazing. Have I told you lately that I think you're living the best life? Look at this view! The pool! Gah! One day, you were signing with TCA and we were celebrating. Next thing I knew, you were introduced to Liam and all our lives changed forever."

After many more one-on-one classes, Ana was finally able to float. She let the water support her as she drifted in the pool, eyes closed behind her sunglasses, a smile on her face.

"I know. It *is* amazing. How does that even happen for me? For us?"

"It happened. Real life facts. Now you moved in with your beau and offered me the best job in the world, and I'm basking in the glow of your sun. As one should. There's enough sunlight to share, right? 'Cuz I'm so happy, basking around. Basking hard."

Eyes still closed, Ana grinned wide. "That's just California life, my friend."

"No, I mean Liam is the sun and it's making all of this possible for all of us." Ely splashed a few drops of water on Ana.

Ana ignored it. "He'd hate it if you called him the sun."

Ely sighed. "I know he would. But he's so darn optimistic—you know, *sunny*— about everything and, well, it was him coming into our lives that changed everything, right?"

"We could argue I came into his life and, as I come with a package, it's changing your life, too."

"Oooh. I like your version better. *You* came into *his* life and made it amazing. He should be thankful every day."

Ana laughed. "We didn't start Jump Cannon Productions for the purpose of getting you here... but I'm so, so happy it worked out that way."

The doorbell ringtone blared from Ana's phone, prompting her to stand in the pool and stare at it for a second, stunned. Ely turned to Ana and they gazed at each other for another beat. The ringtone went off again just as Ely shrugged.

"Liam wouldn't be ringing the doorbell." Ana scrambled out of the pool and checked her phone. She unlocked it with the idea of checking the gate camera, but her attention went to her text notifications first.

> Liam: Sorry, I'm going
> to be ab an hr late

"Okay," Ana mumbled before tapping on the security app.

Someone stood outside, dispassionately looking around and glancing at the camera. Ana gasped. She tapped on the little button with the mic on it, which let her talk to the person at the gate.

"Alex?!" she called, hearing the surprise in her voice.

"Ana?" he asked, his eyes zeroing on the camera. "Hey."

Ana grabbed her phone tight in her still-wet hands. "I didn't know you'd come! Everything okay?"

His lips pursed. "It'd be better if I could come in."

"Crap, yes, of course!" She tapped the *open gate* button. "Come in, just make sure the gate closes behind you."

Ana watched him go back to his car to drive in, before she grabbed her coverup from one of the sunbathing chairs.

"Did I hear right?" Ely said still from the pool, arms crossed over the warm tile. "Is Alex here?"

Ana nodded. "Yes, I— I don't even know, Ely."

Ana made her way to the door while tapping furiously on her phone.

> Ana: Alex is here at
> home. Did he tell
> you he was coming?

Not expecting a reply in the one second it'd take her to open the door, she carried her phone in her hand. She reached the door and opened it, her wet hair dripping on her back.

Alex took what seemed like a traveling bag from the back of the car; he closed the trunk door with a loud *slam!* before he approached the house's entrance.

"Hi, Alex!" Ana said, letting him in. "This is a surprise."

He shrugged. "It's been about a month since you and Liam offered me the job. I need to talk to you both, see what I'd be getting into."

Alex didn't try to kiss her cheek, let alone hug her; he walked into the house and Ana closed the door behind them.

"You're lucky we're here." Ana followed him; he stopped in the middle of the room and dropped his bag on the floor. He gazed around the space. "I just arrived a couple of days ago, and Liam is on his way."

"Yeah. He texted me a few days ago and mentioned he'd be here today."

"Hello," Ely said as she came into the house.

Ana tore her attention away from Alex to admire Ely's entrance, and she had to press her lips together not to smile. Ely walked with confidence, her cover up open and waving behind her. The soft curves of her belly and hips echoed her steps with small earthquakes on her flesh, and her eyes shone with mischief. Curious, Ana studied Alex's reaction. All he did was lift an eyebrow and sweep a look up and down Ely.

"Hi," he said, his voice neutral.

"I'm Ely." She extended a hand forward. "Ana's best friend. Also known as Elena Castillo, the new Manager of Social Impact for Jump Cannon Productions."

Ely had said her name and position full of pride, and with the Spanish pronunciation of her name. Alex was slow to respond, but his hand came up to shake Ely's. He didn't say anything.

"You're Liam's brother," Ely added, explaining for him. He nodded once. Ely arched an eyebrow.

"Well, you're staying here, right?" Ana asked, breaking the silent battle building between them. "Ely is taking the guest room but we have another room with a bed, it's just not as finished."

"If that's okay." Alex bent to pick up his bag.

"Of course it's okay." Ana pointed the way with a head slant. "Come this way."

"I'm going to change," Ely announced.

Ana showed Alex his room; he decided he wanted to rest a bit, so she left him. When Ana checked her phone right before showering, she saw Liam's response.

Liam: WTF? omw

She shook her head for the thousandth time at his abbreviations, a smile on her face nonetheless.

———

Liam opened the door to his home and it struck him— his life was very different to what it had been eighteen months ago. Where it used to be a safe but lonely place, now three people were in it: his girlfriend, her best friend and now employee, and his brother. There was love, life... and conflict.

He'd pressed his lips at the thought, but they relaxed into a soft smile when the first person he saw was Ana.

She happened to be walking from the rooms to the kitchen. She caught sight of him and the relief on her face made his heart flutter. She needed him. She found comfort in him.

She detoured and came to him, instead. She hugged him when he closed the door behind him.

"I'm so glad you're here." She reached up to kiss him. "Did you get my text? He's still in his room."

He left his small suitcase and the bag full of promotional gifts on the floor, before grabbing her by the waist.

"I saw it when I got in the car. He didn't tell me he'd come... did he say anything?"

"That he wanted to talk to us about working for the company."

"Okay," he began, before Ely interrupted them.

"I just caught my bosses necking. Do we have an HR department I can report things to?" Ely gave Liam a humor-filled smirk. "Hi, Liam."

He let go of Ana to give Ely a quick hug. "So you met Alex."

"Yeah, he makes an impression," she said, pulling her smile to the side.

"I wasn't trying to." Alex's words cut into the space.

They all turned to stare at Alex, who crossed his arms, and whose face remained impassive and unimpressed. If Liam wasn't mistaken, his eyes were sweeping the room, looking at his paintings on the walls, but showing no reaction.

"It's good to see you." Liam refused to spend too long thinking about how he'd hugged Ely but not his own brother. "We weren't expecting you."

Alex stared at Liam, for once giving him his eyes. Even so, his brother's eyes were shuttered and there wasn't much of a spark in them. "I thought I'd risk it. I arrived earlier today and looked around the city, seeing if I can see myself here."

"What did you think?" Ana stepped closer to Liam and put an arm around his waist.

Alex glanced at Ely but settled on the ceiling. "I think I want to have a few meetings with you, see what could happen if I said yes."

Liam nodded. "We weren't sure we were going to hear from you, so we put out some feelers for the position but, if you want to talk more about it, that'd be great."

Alex squinted, his lips pursing. "That's smart."

"We want to be smart," Liam said.

Ana stole a glance at Liam that told him his tone had been a bit more tense than he'd intended.

"Well, let's make dinner, shall we?" Ana said.

Chapter Nine

LIAM HID IN HIS and Ana's bedroom the next morning, only a little embarrassed by it. He sat on the bed, scrolling his phone as he waited for Ana to be done showering. He'd wanted to gather fortitude before having to face the day.

After an awkward and frustrating dinner the night before, Ana had let him vent in their room before sleeping. Once spent of his rancor, she held him until his heart warmed up. Then she'd let him make love to her and fall asleep in her arms.

Now, anger gone, all that was left was fear.

He looked up when Ana stepped into their room, steam escaping out of their bathroom and trailing behind her like a faint cloud. She'd wrapped her hair in a towel and another one covered her body.

She startled upon seeing him. She placed a hand on her heart. "Oh! Liam! You scared me."

"Sorry." He stood and got in her way. He smiled, his hands settling on her waist automatically.

"You okay?" She asked, putting her free hand on his chest.

"Yeah. Just not looking forward to spending all morning alone with Alex."

Liam would stay home with his brother, while Ely and Ana went out looking for apartments for Ely. Alex and Liam were going to join them in the afternoon, when they started shopping for office space.

To her credit, Ana didn't laugh at him. "If things get tough, you could join us earlier than you thought. That way, even if he complains about having to look at places for Ely, at least we can all try to deal with it together. As a team."

He angled his head to kiss her. "You're the best. I'm sure we'll be fine."

"I'm sure too but if he grabs a knife or anything, don't hesitate to call me."

He laughed. "Please tell me again you don't think I'm— we're— making a mistake by offering him the position."

She sighed. "I don't know if we are, to be honest, but we won't know unless he says yes. You've seen the other resumés; they all look about the same as his. He doesn't have a lot of experience in the film industry but neither does Ely and we're okay with that. They can learn, right?"

"He's such a grump, though!" he hissed. "What if he makes it hard to work with him? For Ely, especially."

"Answer me this question. Do you think he's professional? Would he jeopardize Jump Cannon out of— I don't know, pettiness?"

Liam frowned. "No. I don't think so. He's difficult but he's honorable. I think."

Ana tightened the towel around her body but took off the one wrapping her hair. She combed her wet tendrils with her fingers.

"So that's an advantage we have with him we don't have with other candidates. People we've been chatting with have been on their best behavior; we don't know what they're like when they're being assholes. And we don't know if they're honorable."

Liam chuckled. "Okay, yeah. I see your point."

"We're gonna be taking a risk no matter who we pick. If Alex says yes and we go with him, well... at least we don't have to be polite when we ask him to chill the fuck out and do better."

With a relieved smile settling on his lips, Liam brought Ana close to him, arms around her waist and hands down on her ample ass. It not being enough, he scrunched the towel up to get it out of the way, and filled his hands with soft, naked, generous flesh.

"You smell amazing," he said.

Ana arched an eyebrow. "And I need to get ready to go out with Ely. She'll threaten to break up with me if I'm late. She's looking forward to this."

"Okay, okay. I'll go." He gave her a resigned sigh.

He stole one more kiss before getting out of their bedroom, a smile on his face, confidence grounding his step.

Chapter Ten

THE NEXT FEW DAYS went by in a flash. Three days before Liam and Ana were scheduled to fly to Toronto, they signed a lease for their office space and were busy planning the set up. As they did all of that, Liam couldn't help but be optimistic. Alex seemed to be really considering this option. He'd been giving opinions about what might work for an office space, and peppered them with questions about the company as they drove around the city. Grumbling, but he'd participated.

That night, they had decided to attend a restaurant opening. Jen was a much better fit for Liam than Coulton ever was but, one thing Jen had in common with his old agent, was her insistence that he get seen. Once in a while, Jen and the PR team would pull their strings and set up a thing or two for him to go to. Lately, Liam had made them all very happy by requesting for events himself.

Networking was a lot easier when he did it with a personal purpose.

Holding hands with Ana, he greeted people he knew, and moved through the big open room slowly. He didn't get a chance to study the decor details, but the soft warm light and bassy electronic music made for a sultry atmosphere. People milled around the place, with an impressive mural of LA as the back-drop, a mixed media piece in different textures and the skyline in metal. He introduced both Ana and Ely and casually mentioned Jump Cannon every chance he got; Alex had escaped them, finding their table and hiding on his phone.

After half an hour of socializing, Liam, Ana, and Ely joined him.

"That was great!" Ely's smile shone across the table. "I'm so glad to have you as a trailblazer, Liam. Without your contacts this would be a mountain to climb."

He nodded. "Without my contacts, this would be almost im-possible. But I do know people, and Ana is amazing at what she does, so I think we have an actual shot at this."

Ana's eyes sparkled, her smile generous. She leaned into him and kissed his cheek. "What you and I do is only half of the equation."

"What I've gathered to date about the structure of the compa-ny is a smart strategy, too, I think," Alex said to Liam's surprise. "You can bring other producers on board or keep it small; either way, it's scalable."

"They are smart people, Sandy." Ely smirked in Alex's direc-tion. Liam had to bite his lips at her nickname for Alex. At some point in the past three days, Ely had started calling him *Sandy*. Liam wasn't sure why or when it had happened, but he knew his brother had to hate it. It was probably the reason she used it. Ely gazed at Ana and Liam instead. "I'm so excited for everything we can do with Jump Cannon."

Alex rolled his eyes but said nothing. "Is the Manager of Operations expected to go network, too?"

"Yes, especially when Liam and I are not available," Ana replied. "Especially in the beginning."

Alex nodded and stared at a water fixture nearby. A server came to take their orders for food and drinks, and bring water for them all.

"So, what's next?" Ely asked once they were gone.

"Ana and I need to prep for the premiere and other events in Toronto." Liam sipped some water. "You will stay at our place, of course, until you're ready to move and your parents get here with your stuff. We signed the lease for the office we chose effective tomorrow; Mo will pick up the keys and bring them to us."

"We'll get the place furnished over the weekend." Ana directed her words at Ely. "But you'll have to be on call to help handle that stuff. You know, handle calls from the movers if they need anything. The way we organized it, they're taking all the stuff into the office on Saturday and, on Sunday, they will be there to move things around according to your directions. They won't do much with the decor, though."

"Sounds good." Ely nodded. "My top priority is to get an assistant. I'll focus on that tomorrow morning and on Monday. I have three finalists for the role, and I'll need someone helping me out next week."

"I'll be able to help you once we're back from Toronto," Ana said.

"I had to pack next week full of meetings, after we return from Canada." Liam reached for Ana's hand on the table, squeezing it to gain resolve. He glanced at Alex. "Mostly virtual, but still a lot of my time is tied up. I can help randomly, here and there, but perhaps it's best if you pretend I won't be there for most of it... though Alex might be."

Silence landed around them. Ely and Ana turned to study Alex as well. Liam's stomach knotted up, just as Ana comforted him by turning her hand, interlocking fingers with his, and squeezing back. They needed Alex's answer, and the question of his participation was implicit in Liam's words.

"Let's imagine I say yes," Alex said and Ely groaned. Liam would have found humor in the exchange at any other time, but not while he waited with baited breath. "I'd have to sign the contract with Carruthers, then meet with Elena a bunch of times, create a few drafts for the way both our departments would interact, and then all of us get together to finalize the structure, right?"

"Right." Liam stared at his brother, a frown weighing his eyebrows down. "C'mon. It's a good opportunity for you. I think you'd be great for it... and I'd like to have you around."

Alex pursed his lips. "I hate all the Hollywood stuff."

They all waited for him to add more, to relent and give them an answer.

Alex took a deep, strained sigh. "I'm sending my immediate resignation to my employer tomorrow. If they haven't made it clear they intend to fire me, yet. I've been gone for a few days which I'm sure didn't land well with them."

Liam, Ana, and Ely watched him without a word; Liam caught himself holding his breath. Even though he'd uttered the words, a little voice in his head doubted their veracity. Perhaps Liam had gotten it wrong.

Silence continued around them, growing heavier with every passing second. Alex arched an eyebrow in challenge, not caring that things were getting awkward.

"Does that mean you're taking the job?"

Ana had been the first to speak, putting Liam's question into words. Alex didn't respond right away; Liam's attention stayed focused on his brother.

Alex spoke to Ana, as if he could pretend she was the only one at the table. "I wouldn't be quitting my current job if I didn't have something lined up. Your business plan looks solid. There's a good balance between the for profit side and the social side. I think there are some things that will need adjusting, but that can come with time. If you still plan to be flexible with it for the first year."

"We still plan for it to be flexible," Ana said. "But I think at this point we also need a concrete answer... tell us you're taking *this* job. With the three of us."

Alex kept his eyes on Ana, and Liam was thankful for it for the first time. He believed that, were Alex to look back at him, he'd see the vulnerability Liam felt, clear in his eyes.

Alex tapped a finger on the table. "I'm assuming the plan is to have an strategic meeting per trimester for the first year, at the least. Probably two. You should add that specifically to the plan, so that it doesn't fall through the cracks."

"That was always the plan. Like we've said before—" Ely started, but Alex interrupted her.

Alex gazed at the water feature again, but responded to Ely. "Still, you should have a meeting per month, at least, with your peer. Keeping things on track."

"I'll be sure to keep my *peer* on track." Liam wasn't used to hearing Ely irritated, but her voice tended to change when she talked to Alex. "Now, is that peer going to be you, Sandy? Yes or no answer."

His heart beating fast, Liam waited for confirmation.

Alex flicked a hand between Liam and Ana. "Unless you've changed your minds, yes, I'm taking the offer."

This time, their silence only lasted three heartbeats.

"Welcome on board!" Ana said, reacting first once more.

A mix of dread and hope flooded Liam's heart, and he'd have stayed quiet hadn't Ana's foot tapped on his shin.

"Yes," Liam said, "I'm glad. I know you will be amazing in this role."

He could only hope those were more than vacuous words.

Chapter Eleven

LIAM HAD TRIED TO prepare Ana for the whirlwind to come, but he doubted she knew exactly what to expect. She'd been to a couple of big events with him, and she'd been to film festivals before, but not one this big, and not while with him. He had the experience to know how things changed when you were this well known. He could only hope he and Ana would sail through the storm victorious and with not too many bumps.

The plane landed and he and Ana were made to wait in it for a bit but, after about twenty minutes, they made their way out, holding hands. He preferred having the small connection with her at all times; it comforted him.

"I'm still not used to flying privately," she said next to him, shaking her head. "Seems like such a waste of resources."

"You know why we do it," he began, but she interrupted.

"Yes, I know. I'm still shaken by it, that's all."

"Liam, Ms. Lira, good evening." Becca, Liam's publicist— who would work with Ana for the weekend— greeted them at the door of the private hanger. "If you'll follow me, I'll tell you about the plans for the next few days. Your luggage is already on the way to your hotel room."

"Call me Ana, please."

"Sure thing, Ana," Becca replied, while guiding them through and out of the building.

A driver waited for them. They got in the car without speaking. The two sets of passenger seats faced each other, and Ana sat next to him on one and Becca in front of them on the other. The car began to move.

Becca reviewed her tablet, quickly tapping through. "Okay, you have a packed schedule, which should surprise nobody. Did you receive the agenda to your emails?"

"Yeah," Liam said while Ana nodded. "We talked about it on the flight here."

"Excellent. As you know, the festival is Thursday through Monday. You came here a day late but that should work well, you don't need to rush for opportunities. Social media shows people are waiting for you so that's great."

"Any thoughts on the film yet? Reactions to the trailer and stuff you've seen?" Ana asked.

"More of the same. People are focusing a lot on your relationship more than on whether it's a fair portrayal of Hollywood or not. That's actually good. We really want to put you two at the center of attention whenever you're in public. Make you look strong but also a mystery, because you never talk about your relationship. That could romanticize any negative reactions from the documentary which, in all honesty, we hope won't be too bad. Just be ready for the paparazzi and fans; remember everyone has a camera with them and assume someone will be taking pictures."

"I thought the plan was to make a clear separation between our relationship and the film?" Ana leaned her shoulder against Liam's arm. "To bring the focus to the themes rather than the romance."

Becca lifted a shoulder in a dismissive manner. "That's the official response, yes, and definitely keep to that when talking to people, but it won't actually manage what people are saying—they'll say whatever they want and what they seem to care about is the romance. So it's better if we have a plan to use it, rather than be at the mercy of it."

"I don't want people thinking Liam's initial bitterness makes him entitled, or ungrateful. Have you seen anything like that?"

"No. We've been trying to frame all of that as something in the past, and so far most people are taking it at face value."

"And it is the truth, that's in the past." Liam let go of Ana's hand and put his arm around her shoulders. "People will keep doing what they've been doing for the past year. So we let them and hope it'll drown any negative comments."

Becca nodded. "Reviews will likely have a mix of both, but word of mouth? It should be mostly positive."

Ana sighed. "Okay."

They fell into silence as Becca got busy with her tablet. The city passed them by, the car keeping a decent speed.

Becca closed her tablet in its protective folder. "Then we're good. Everything seems to be going smoothly, all events confirmed and the documentary premiere is going well on schedule for Sunday. I recommend you two go out for dinner tonight, get seen."

"We plan to." Liam checked his watch. "Mo said he'd get us reservations."

"He did." She got to her tablet again, just as their car drove into the hotel's parkade. "He probably sent you the info already, but I'll send it again so you have it readily available."

"Thanks."

"Any questions?"

Liam and Ana shook their heads as the car parked next to the elevator. They all got out and into the lift in silence; Becca left them at the Lobby level, assuring them that Mo had made it to Toronto earlier and had checked in for them already. They went up to their suite directly.

After Mo helped them set up, gave them keys, and did a general check in, he left to give them privacy.

Ana gave a big sigh; she slumped a bit as she approached the big windows overlooking the city.

He came close to her, placing a hand on her lower back. "You okay?"

"I am... for now."

"It's a lot, I know."

"You've told me, but... I managed to keep away from the worst of it over the last year and I was— I am— looking forward to this fest. I hope the busyness of it doesn't rob me of what I want from it."

"Yeah, me too. My experience is that these events are like a blur but… maybe we can have something different together."

She opened the window and stepped onto the small terrace. He followed her.

She nodded as she studied the sights. "Connect with the fans, take the publicity opportunities for you to keep your success and for my name to get better known. Networking for the company and helping each other survive it all. We can do this."

Wind lifted tendrils of Ana's hair, messing it up. With his free hand, he pulled it back and kept it away from her face with as much gentleness as he could.

"We're gonna do fine," he said, giving her a kiss. "We're gonna be fine."

She gave him one of her glorious smiles, eyes soft. Surprising him, she took her phone out and took a picture of them against the city skyline.

Turning in his arms, she opened her social media app and he watched over her shoulder how she made a post with it.

#Imlucky, she wrote.

—

Ana took a deep breath and prepared for the long walk ahead. Even though it would likely take her only ten minutes to get to the restaurant if she were alone, it would probably take a lot longer with Liam. They had never gone out and about that way, where he might get recognized, but he said things were different during a fest like this. That people expected him to.

They left an hour before their reservation time; they had invited Michael, the man who almost replaced Alex as the managing head for Jump Cannon for dinner and didn't want to be late. If the production company grew solid and expanded, they wanted to have a good standing relationship with the man, in case he was the right person to bring into the company.

It took only a few steps out of the hotel for a small group to stop her and Liam. The young women wanted pictures, and they asked Ana to be the photographer. After interacting with that group, she and Liam continued walking, hand in hand, until a different group stopped them at the intersection.

She didn't think much about it the first few times it happened, but soon a pattern became evident: people didn't seem to care about her. She tried to stay friendly and ignore the random seething looks she received, telling herself this was to be expected.

Someone asked, "Are you his assistant?"

Ana turned to the woman, admiring her pink hair and pushing her own irritation down.

"No. I directed him for Limelight, premiering this Sunday."

"Oh! You're Ana Lira! You're his girlfriend! Can we take a picture?"

All traces of irritation disappeared within her. Ana's smile turned authentic. "Sure!"

A couple of the people conglomerating around Liam watched them take the picture, but no one else approached.

"Okay, see you around, everyone," Liam announced. He approached Ana and took her hand. "We really appreciate the support!"

He leaned to her as they resumed their walk and whispered, "Hungry? We'll make it to the restaurant eventually."

"I'm quite hungry, actually."

"We're just a block away."

He kissed her temple. They only stopped for pictures with fans another three times in the last block.

Chapter Twelve

BECCA SAT DOWN WITH them the next morning for breakfast.

"Fans definitely adore you," she said. Ana wasn't completely sure that it was a plural you. She'd had a short call with Reagan earlier in the morning, who'd suggested she try to find her own fans, rather than share in Liam's. "So far, most of the conversation online is positive. People coming across you two think you're adorable together, so that'll help boost the documentary's reception."

Liam nodded.

Becca tapped on her tablet and showed them the screen. "This is a picture of the two of you from last night, you kissing her temple, that is doing the rounds. You look like you adore her and stole a moment with her."

So no, not a plural you. Which Ana got, Becca was his publicist primarily, after all.

She wished she could convince herself she didn't mind. Then she wouldn't have to work so hard at ignoring the cinder of irritation lodged in her diaphragm.

"Fair assessment," Liam responded to Becca, squeezing Ana's hand.

"Today it's Ana's panel, Women Directors in Filmmaking," Becca continued. She turned to Ana. "Did you get my email with the prep document? It was cleared by Reagan."

"Yeah, I did."

"Did you get a chance to read it?"

Ana nodded. "I did, this morning."

"Excellent. Liam, this is your pass." She handed him a lanyard. "You can either wait for Ana in the green room, or watch from the sides."

"Do you think you'll be distracting if you're there, Liam?" Ana modulated her voice to sound casual, as much as it was in her power to do so. "Reagan is worried you're getting all the attention and I'm falling to the side. She told me to make sure I get some attention as well."

He arched his eyebrows. "I'll do my best to be inconspicuous."

"What are you planning to wear to the panel?" Becca asked Ana.

She looked down at herself; faded black jeans and a Madonna shirt, a black-and-white stencil poster of her 80s look, with bright red lips. "This?"

"Mhh. Would you consider wearing a bright red lipstick like on the shirt? And another layer of mascara, if you don't want to bother with fake lashes. Maybe a heavy, long necklace, something that's going to rest between your boobs to accentuate them? And studded, black leather bracelets, if we want to go with this kind of look."

It took Ana a few seconds to respond. "I... I don't have bracelets like that."

"I'll get you some." Without skipping a beat, Becca started typing on her tablet to get things done.

Ana turned to Liam, breathless, eyes open wide.

He squeezed her hand again and kept it tight in his. "It's just posturing. Just for show in interviews and such."

"As your now casual publicist," Becca added, eyes still glued to her tablet, "it's part of my job to help with the... posturing."

Ana gulped. "Right."

"It's like for the industry events you go to with me," Liam added. "No different than jewelry you wouldn't normally wear, but do because it looks better with a fancy dress."

"I thought you would have gotten used to stuff like this after a year." Becca lifted her eyes to Ana. "Unless Liam has been protecting you from the worst of it?"

"I wouldn't call it that," Liam replied. "I'd avoid it for myself, too, if I could. If you'd let me, Becca."

The publicist smirked. "And I'd let you, if you said my job is to keep you happy, which I don't think it is."

"Fine, fine. I know you're doing your job."

"And you let me because you know I'm good at it." Becca winked and excused herself.

Ana couldn't help but notice that they had resolved the situation between them, and Ana hadn't gotten much of a say.

———

Ana had attended panels as a guest before, but never one with over four hundred people in the audience.

She waited backstage, close to the wings. As the host introduced the panel and started calling their names, her co-panelists stepped into the light and onto the stage, waving and exchanging a few words with the host. Ana had been told she'd be called to the stage second-to-last; she passed the time by grounding herself in Liam's words.

She'd left him in the green room and, right as she stepped away, he'd brought her close to him and whispered in her ear.

"Your brilliance is all you need. You'll rock this thing."

Then he'd kissed her and settled on the couch there, watching her go with a producer.

She sighed, smiling. She could still feel his kiss on her lips.

"Next, let us welcome someone having a bit of a breakthrough moment," the host announced. "I'm sure many of us know her name from her past projects and have gotten used to hearing her name more and more around filmmaking circles. She's a producer, director, and editor, Miss Ana Lira!"

She stepped onto the stage and walked to her chair, grin wide and a casual wave toward the audience. The host kept introducing her as she sat down and got more comfortable.

"With a handful of documentaries out there, people are coming to know Ana Lira's brand of intimate, genuine close ups of people. She gets to know them and understand them as we do, and then she shares the result with us. Ana," the host said, turning to her now. "For those of us in the indie sphere, it's well-known that we expect to see your name getting renown and awards any time now. Your latest project dives deep into the life of a big name in Hollywood, and rumors say it's your most daring film yet. Would you agree with that?"

"It is daring, yes, because it challenges the ideals of glamor we have of someone living in the limelight. Not everyone wants their bubble burst, you know? But it was important to tell the truth."

"I'm sure that makes everyone's antennas tingle— can't wait to discuss the power of truth during our panel! Thanks, Ana. Now, for our last but not least panelist, let's welcome Rossana Levy!"

Ana exchanged a few words with the panelist already sitting to her side, before she scanned the auditorium. The lights made it difficult to see details, casting everyone attending in the shade. A narrow, short table with water bottles and name plates held the space for Ana and the other filmmakers and, to the side, the host stood at a podium.

The panel started with general questions open to Ana and the other guests, all about the editing and directing process. They got to chat and compare processes, and the host did a good job at keeping the mood light. Laughing with everyone made her comfortable.

"The point is to convince the audience that they want to watch what you're offering. You need to know your niche to do that." Nina, another panelist whose clip they were discussing, said.

"Absolutely," Ana commented. "Convincing them they're lucky they're watching your film."

"When really, we're lucky they want to watch it!" Rossana added, and they all laughed.

"You've said many times, Ana, that you answer a question in your films. Tell us a bit more about that?"

"Sure, yeah, that's how I structure my documentaries. As I get to know the person, what is the number one question I have about who they are? About their life?"

"You must tag scenes heavily," Diwa, the last panelist, added.

"I do! I do." Ana gathered her hair and pulled it all over one shoulder. "It's almost like, the question comes as a result of the connections I make, then all the pieces of the answer form a... a... polygon?" They all laughed. "And I straighten that out to tell the story. The final edit is always about, a, making sure the story makes sense and, b, that it's gripping enough. If I want you to hear the answer, I need to convince you that you have the same question."

"That's a perfect segway!" The host said. "It's time for your clip. Can you tell us a bit about what we're going to see?"

"I decided to keep it simple and share the first three minutes of the film. You'll see Liam— " cheers erupted from the audience; Ana smiled. "I know, right? You'll see him in contrast: the Liam McMillan you know and the Liam McMillan he is when there are no cameras around... well, except for mine, as I could capture him."

"Sounds promising! Let's watch."

Ana knew what was going to show on the screen above the panel, but she turned to watch it regardless.

First, a warning: there would be flashes of light throughout the film, recommending precautions for photosensitive viewers. The screen faded to black for one, two seconds, before darkness was broken by multiple camera flashes, all lighting up the screen in quick succession. A shot of Liam on the red carpet appeared first, wearing an impeccable suit, captivating smile, and shining emerald eyes. Screams of fans and reporters vyed for his attention.

The screen faded black again, just for an instant, before scenes of him floating in the pool at his home filled the shot, quiet all around. Another scene, now of him lounging on his sofa, face uninterested. More flashes, then a series of superposed scenes of interviews he'd done drew the attention... Ana had had to pay the largest sums she'd ever paid for rights to use those in her film. The sequence ended on a wide shot of him walking alone alongside the cliffs of the California coast, tan, broad back bare, the ocean infinite to his side. He looked small. Before the scene ended, Ana's voice filled the space.

"He's extremely busy, all the time. From what I've gathered, if he's not filming on location, he has training and meetings all the time. If he's home, he's *home*." Ana's face appeared on screen. It was a shot she'd recorded the day before they went on their road trip, right after arriving at his— now their— home in LA. "I saw him work today. Video and phone calls for hours on end. From a brief chat with his PA, this is just a tiny sample of his every day. No wonder he's said he barely leaves this place... and why it seems he put so much care in its design."

The scene changed once more, this time portraying a shot of Liam walking into the ocean. Ana's voice filled the room again. "He seems lonely."

A final fade to black, and the lights filled the auditorium in warm light again.

Ana's heart beat fast. While she expected the applause— was grateful for it— she was surprised by the murmuring that seemed to accompany it.

She turned back to the audience, her eyes tracking the space. Despite the shining stage lights hiding most attendant details, she'd recognize his size and presence anywhere. Liam leaned against the wall, a few paces away from the stage, and people noticed him there. Her gut reacted to him, too; for the first time ever, a flurry of mixed feelings made its way through her.

"He didn't stay alone for long, at least," Nina joked and everyone laughed. Ana smiled, ignoring the discomfort in her stomach.

"Wow, what a start!" The host checked his notes. "Thanks for sharing that. Can you tell us, how different was it to work with Liam McMillan than with your other subjects? You went from a teacher in the most remote corner of Australia, talking about resources and indigenous rights, to one of the most famous actors in the world. How do you even get connected with someone like him?"

"It wasn't easy to connect with Marlee, the teacher, either." Ana hoped her grin hid her displeasure at the question. "But getting to work with Liam involved a lot of luck. I was offered the opportunity and I took it right away. Aside from how fortuitous it was to meet him, working with him wasn't any different, really."

"How did you manage the romance between you two?" the host continued, his eyes sweeping over the audience as if they were in on the question. "Because, based on what you've shared about your process, you either had to include that in the movie or risk losing objectivity."

Ana curled a hand into a fist on her lap, hidden from everyone under the table. She kept her smile. "Liam and I have made a point not to discuss our relationship publicly, but I can say that we didn't get together until after we were done filming the documentary. In the movie itself, I left everything that was relevant to answering the central question. You'll have to watch it and make your own mind about whether you think you see romance there as well or not."

"We're professional," Diwa said. Ana turned to her co-panelist and prayed that, whatever she said, it helped to keep the conversation grounded in their work, rather than Ana's boyfriend. "This work is serious business to us."

"Absolutely." Relief sparkled in Ana's chest. "The material consequences of people's reaction to this film are magnitudes higher than any of my other films because of Liam's fame. Regardless of our relationship and when it started and whether it ever ends, even after we're gone, or done, this documentary will continue to exist because it'll exist forever. It exists before the relationship we have and will be there long after, even if it's in an archive box in a dusty corner of a library. I would never risk my objectivity."

Rossana nodded. "We care about our craft too much to risk objectivity, for whichever reason. Even a handsome man with piercing green eyes."

Everyone laughed, and the topic moved on.

Ana glanced around the auditorium; it seemed Liam had left the room. Relief made an appearance again, quickly followed by guilt: she'd never been glad to not have him near.

She didn't want to feel that way. And yet, when every other question she received was about Liam instead of her work as a director, the heavy weight of his fame impacting her settled in the pit of her stomach, full of jagged edges.

Chapter Thirteen

AFTER THE PANEL, LIAM and Ana attended a cocktail event to network and, after that, a VIP hang at an exclusive bar with several of the producers from the initial event. He and Ana didn't return to the hotel until much later.

Liam was exhausted but, seeing how Ana threw herself to bed face down, maybe she was doing worse. She seemed boneless; her hair a splayed, messy halo all around.

"Tired?" Liam asked. He stood in the middle of the room, watching her.

Ana grunted. The annoying pressure in the pit of his stomach relaxed a little at the domesticity of it.

He reached for the top button of his shirt. "Remember that first time, when you went back to Bloomington after filming and I went on a tour? How I would call you when I got to my hotel room?"

Ana turned on the bed, her listless body minimizing movement, and her arms fell wherever they'd followed her torso. Her hair covered most of her face.

"You must have been really into me," she said, voice gruff.

His lips curled and the pressure in his gut released further. He unbuttoned his shirt, hands slow as he approached her. She lifted a hand to clear the hair off her face, revealing twinkling eyes.

"Does it make you want to gloat?" He pulled at the sides of his shirt to reveal more of his chest to her admiring eyes.

She bit her lips. Her eyes followed his hands. "Yeah."

"Do you want me to take off my shirt?" He wet his bottom lip. She bit hers. "Yeah."

He didn't take off his shirt. He unbuttoned his jeans and crawled into the bed, laying down beside her.

Elbow bent, he rested his head on his hand. "Are you into me?"

"Yeah. Very."

He lifted a hand and followed the long chain of her necklace from her solar plexus up, in between her breasts, and to her neck. He caressed the soft skin with the pad of his index finger, testing the strength of her pulse there.

"How much?" He searched for every piece of her answer she'd give him.

She considered him, eyes roaming over his face, down his torso.

"This is where I wish I knew poetry, because nothing else would suffice."

The knot in his stomach fully released for the first time in hours.

He leaned down to kiss her, softly, exploring. Her stomach growled. He grinned against her lips.

"How about we order some food?" He asked. "Sounds like you could use a bit more today."

"You're perfect." She sighed. "A snack would be great. I drank more than I ate today."

He laughed. "I'll feed you in exchange for more of these adoring eyes you're bestowing on me."

"I'm bestowing you with adoring eyes?"

He nodded, still grinning. "We'll eat, then get cozy in bed, then we'll sleep."

She kissed his cheek and lied back on the bed. Liam took his phone from a nearby table. He sat on the side of the bed, feet planted firmly on the ground. It turned out to be a saving grace, because the email he saw from Alex took his breath away. His heart stopped working.

"What? What happened?" Ana asked. He wasn't sure what had told her something was wrong, but she knew him well enough to notice anyway.

His shoulders slumped low with the weight of the words he read.

"Liam?"

The bed dipped behind him. He twisted in bed as she reached him, a hand on his shoulder.

He dropped his hands to his lap. "Alex quit."

"What?!"

He gave her his phone and she skimmed over Alex's email. He remembered his words clearly.

Liam (and Ana),

I will keep this short. Over the past several days, we've talked at length about this job opportunity you offered me. While I think I gave it a fair chance and, after in-depth consideration, I agreed to join your company, new matters have come to light and I have decided it's best for me to step down.

It's barely appropriate for me to say I quit, as we didn't go as far as signing anything. Still, out of respect, I thought you deserved to hear it from me, rather than come back and realize I had gone back home. That is, if Elena didn't tell you about it first. You deserve to know that it wasn't the job; I have no doubts your company can succeed. I just think I'm not the right person for it.

Good luck. You'll find someone who will fit well with all of you and your vision.

Best,
Alex

"Best? That's what he says?" Ana dropped the phone to her side on the bed, its screen going black.

"Argh!" Liam got out of the bed and stomped to the middle of the room. He held his head in his hands. "He's so— I can't."

"I can't believe he quit."

He closed his eyes, fingertips digging into his scalp. When he didn't reply, she walked to him and hugged him from the back; she rested her temple where his shoulder met his neck. The only warmth in him radiated from that point, but it didn't quite reach the place his brother wounded in his heart.

"I'm sorry, Liam." She squeezed him in her arms.

"When do I stop trying? I'm so tired. I don't know what to do about Alex anymore."

"That's a big question. We can take some time for you to figure it out. I'll support whatever you want to do." She placed a kiss on his back.

He lowered his hands and rested them on top of hers on his stomach. "We still need to find a COO. We can't wait for that."

"We will find someone. I have no doubt. Perhaps Michael, when we know how to do it without seeming flakey. We'll figure it out."

She kissed between his shoulder blades again and let go. He turned to watch her; she took her phone and connected it to the bluetooth speaker on the bedside table. Soon, Foreigner's *I Don't Want to Live Without You* started playing.

He scoffed a reticent chuckle, though his heart melted in gooey love for Ana.

She came to him and wrapped her arms around his naked waist, under his open shirt. Getting as close to him as she could, she put her head on the crook of his neck and started swaying. He wrapped his arms around her, loosely holding hands against her back.

"I can't dance my problems with Alex away—" he started saying but she interrupted.

"We can try."

He shook his head but smiled. "What I was going to say, is that I can't dance those problems away... but that you are here, with me, dancing to Foreigner singing to us about love... this is what I wanted. Exactly this."

She kissed the hollow space between his clavicles. "I want to comfort you when you're hurting, Liam."

He sighed. "We'll get through this. I feel like I can conquer the world, now that I have this at the core."

She lifted her eyes to gaze at him. "We'll conquer it together. But not in a colonizer way."

He chuckled. "Thanks for letting me know you. For listening when I asked you to choose me."

"It was inevitable. You let me know you, too."

Chapter Fourteen

WHILE LIAM ORDERED BREAKFAST to their room, Ana texted
Ely to vent about Alex.

> Ana: did you hear
> what Alex did?!!!
> He QUIT

> Ana: Poor Liam is
> furious. I think he's
> feeling betrayed

Ely didn't reply right away, so Ana got busy setting up a few
things for the day. An hour later, she and Liam sat at the small
table in the room, in the same clothes they'd slept in, reading
news and social media on their phones.

Ana stopped reading her emails when she saw the notification
announcing Ely's text.

Ely: Yeah, he told
me last night. He
left LA already
I think

Ana: did you bite his
head off when he
told you? Pls tell
me you did

Ely: at first, but then
we decided to be
mature and talk it out.
We ended on a good
note, I think

Ana: too bad,
I feel like he
deserves war

Ely: I know you're
exaggerating

"What's going on?" Liam asked. "You're typing furiously."

"I'm ranting to Ely about Alex." She gazed at him.

"Oh." His lips pressed together, but his eyes looked sad. It stung in Ana's heart.

Ana dropped her phone on the table and reached for Liam's hand. "Hey. We're going to figure it out. Your relationship with Alex included."

A small smile softened his lips. "Yeah. What did Ely say?"

"She said they talked it out." Ana arched an eyebrow. "Is it weird that I'm surprised?"

That got a chuckle out of him. "If it is, you're not alone. I thought she'd bite his head off."

"Mmmh. Maybe she's keeping her reaction on the down-low, so we don't send the police there."

Liam shook his head. "They weren't that bad."

"In any case." Ana lifted a shoulder and grabbed her phone again. "I'll ask her when we're back in LA."

Ana typed her response to Ely.

> Ana: only a bit.
> I am angry, but
> Liam is hurt

It took a minute for Ely to respond.

> Ely: Poor Liam. Tell
> him we'll figure it

out. I'll reach out
to the old shortlist
tomorrow

                         Ana: I think we want
                               to reach out to
                           Michael, so give us
                             a couple of days

Ely: sure thing

"Okay." Ana sipped from her coffee. "Ely is in the loop. She'll reach out to the shortlist in a couple of days, if we decide not to ask Michael directly."

He nodded, but he didn't seem to pay close attention. "Sounds good. I'm texting with Mo now, prepping for the calls in a bit."

Ana nodded as well and went back to her phone. She had a follow up text from Ely.

Ely: So I know I don't
show you things people
say about the two of
you anymore, unless it's
important, but this could be.
You might want to know

about this one. You don't
want to be surprised
during an interview or
something.

She sent Ana a screenshot summarizing the content: a blurry picture of them the night before, followed by a title: *Ana Lira doesn't think her relationship with Liam McMillan will last. Trouble in Paradise?*

"Fucks' sake," Ana growled. She placed her phone face down on the table and rubbed her forehead with her fingertips, as if it could prevent the headache of it.

Liam stopped with his coffee mug mid-way. "What."

"Some blog is saying I said we're gonna break up."

"Do you know where they got that from?" He finally brought his mug to his lips.

"No." Ana scoffed. "Ely only sent me the start of the post."

Liam raised an eyebrow. "I'm going to guess it was taken out of context."

Ana's hands jerked away from her face. "Of course it was!"

He put his mug back on the table with a deliberate movement. "Then that's all that matters."

He went back to texting Mo, and with a big sigh, Ana went back to texting Ely.

Ana: yeah, I don't
want to be surprised

if someone asks
me about it. Thanks.

Ely: I'm sorry :(

Ana: This isn't shaping
up to be a good day

Ely: I love you
anyway

Ana: I love you too.

Ana: Gtg. I need to get
ready now or we'll
be late to the interviews.

Ely: Good luck <3

Breakfast that Sunday morning turned out to be the only time they had to catch up with life in general. As soon as the food was gone, Ana joined Liam for a virtual meeting with a production team in Europe, which expressed interest in discussing a co-production. After, Liam attended a couple of interviews booked with him alone to discuss multiple projects with which Ana wasn't involved. During that time, she worked with her agent on the phone to prepare for the premiere, and had two interview calls from people around the world.

Knowing that it would take them a long time to prepare for the premiere, Ana and Liam went for an early lunch to a restaurant in the hope to interact with people before the main event. By this point, Ana wasn't surprised anymore that people mostly cared about Liam. The reality was that directors didn't get as much love from fans, despite what Raegan wanted her to believe.

Upon returning to the hotel, they both worked with their stylists and makeup artists to prepare for the red carpet and following party. The festival being somewhat more casual than an awards show, they dressed less formally. Liam wore a charcoal suit, purple shirt and no tie. Ana wore a two-layer dress, with a tight white mini dress, covered in white chiffon embroidered with bold, colorful flowers. Her hair was half-up and half down, curled into romantic waves.

Once ready, they stood face to face admiring each other. Liam's eyes roamed over her, and he lifted a finger to touch one of the bright flowers on a balloon sleeve.

"Gorgeous," he said. "I'd kiss you, but I don't want to ruin your makeup."

She stepped closer to him and gave him a peck on the lips. "I'm wearing long-lasting lipstick."

"Then can I give you a proper kiss?"

She shook her head. "I wish, but let's not push our luck."

"Oh, well." He reached for one of her hands and lifted it to his lips, where he placed a tender kiss on the back of it.

"Sorry to interrupt," Mo said. "We should get going."

Liam checked his watch. "Okay. Let's do this."

Ana's stomach buzzed with adrenaline. She squeezed Liam's hand to the point it had to hurt him, but he didn't complain. He guided her to their car with a big grin on his face and joy shining in his green eyes.

In the car, Becca and Mo reviewed the plan with them.

Liam's publicist took the lead. "This is how the premiere is set up. Liam will get out of the car first, helping Ana out. From there you can chat briefly with fans, sign posters, et cetera, but you should move quickly— assistants will help you with that. Mo and I will trail behind from a safe distance, so as to not distract from the both of you. After the fans, you'll walk the photo section, then move to chat with journalists in the final part. Got it?"

Now near the theater, they reviewed details on the drawn map of the space. The car stopped, and Liam prepared to get out first.

"Ready?" he asked.

Ana nodded. An assistant opened Liam's door; anticipation built inside of her to such high levels she got dizzy— and yet, butterflies took flight all over her inner world.

Liam got out of the car and buttoned his jacket. People screamed and called for him, but he turned to her and offered his hand. She grabbed it and let him help her out of the car, grounding herself in his touch.

Ana's eyes swept the gathering and the short walk to the theater's entrance. Noise still surrounded them, familiar like the times she went with him to award shows the previous year but different, too. Not as loud, not as busy... but many people, and all of them for something that was hers. Her grin broke wide, and Ana wondered if it was possible to be so happy that your very sense of reality shifted.

Liam kissed her temple. "Let's do this," he said in her ear.

Screams multiplied with his gesture. She smiled at him, grateful for his presence, for how he'd opened a door for her and encouraged her to cross it.

He nodded, like he knew what she felt, and smiled back. He held her hand and they walked to the group of fans waiting across a barrier.

"Liam! Liam!"

"Can you sign this?"

"Sure," he said, letting go of her hand and, taking a marker from Becca, signed posters and random merchandise from his movies.

Ana stood beside him, waiting.

"Can we take a selfie?" One of the fans asked him.

"Absolutely." He brought Ana in with an arm around her waist.

"And can we get one of the two of us?" The fan asked.

Liam laughed and posed for it.

Ana took a deep breath, sealing her smile in place as fans kept calling for Liam. She took a few extra steps and tried to find— or make— her own fans.

"Hi!" Ana told someone across the barrier. "Looking forward to the documentary?"

"Yes!" the fan replied. "I heard you get to see the real Liam in it— can't wait!"

"You're the director, right?" Someone else asked. "You're Ana Lira."

"I am."

"You're so pretty," a third person said.

Ana laughed. "Thank you."

Liam joined her and the three fans she'd been engaging with turned to him and asked him for his autograph. Ana moved to the next group.

"Hello," Ana tried with the group. Most people stared at her boyfriend, but she tried not to let it affect her.

"You're Liam's girlfriend!" One of the fans said.

"And his director for this film."

"You're so lucky."

She nodded. "I am, yes."

By the time she'd tried chatting with fans three times, she'd been forced to accept that fans were there for him; that if people followed her career, they treated it differently than his. A fist grabbed her stomach, twisting and telling her she was barely more than Liam's entourage.

Fuck that. So what? Being a director was never about the glamor. She refused to be jealous of Liam's fame... especially when she was extremely aware of its costs.

Becca put an arm around Liam and guided him away from the fans, and both apologized to them. Ana waved at them and followed Liam and Becca. She quickly reminded Ana and Liam about the photo section, how they'd take pictures together and apart. Liam, as usual, managed to make her feel cared for with a simple touch; his presence comforted her, as distracting from her as it was, and even if she wasn't the focus of attention, the movie would gain higher traction thanks to him. She didn't want to forget that.

When pictures were done, Becca called Ana to stand next to Liam at the interviewing section, and to answer questions together.

The group of reporters wasn't as big as the ones at award shows, but much bigger than Ana had ever seen for her movies before. Big for a festival, in any case. Ana took a deep breath, the lingering stress of being faced by flashing cameras and screams for people wanting their attention— too close to the experience of paparazzi for comfort— but finding refuge in standing next to Liam.

Becca led them to the first reporter.

"Hello!" Liam said, his professional, casual smile on, and a hand on the small of her back.

Ana smiled as well. "Hi there."

"Hi, both of you. We're so excited to watch this documentary. There are rumors running around about how it depicts the ugly side of Hollywood. Can you tell us more about that?"

The reporter placed the microphone in front of Liam. Ana made herself smile.

"I wouldn't say it's about the ugly side of it, but the difficult side. Not everything is glam and sparkle and in this film we talked a lot about that."

"And it must not have been easy to jump into the glam of it all. How are you dealing with it?"

It was Ana's turn to speak. "As well as I can. Being around Liam has brought a lot of attention to me as a person that I never expected to experience, and it tends to make my work harder to see for some folks."

The journalist nodded, but a spark of understanding was missing from his eyes.

"One more question. You've said that you worry about backlash from this movie. Can you tell us more about that?"

The microphone went back to Liam.

He frowned. "The nature of the film is to look at Hollywood and what it takes to be involved with huge projects as often as I do, and explore that through a critical lens. While some folks may be curious about it, some others could see it as more cynical and criticize us for it."

"Thank you."

They moved to the next reporter. Ana told herself she'd have a chance to share her vision, yet.

"Hello, guys!" the reporter exclaimed.

"Hi," Ana and Liam responded.

"Thanks for chatting with us. You look gorgeous Ana. Who are you wearing?"

"This dress is by Colombian designer Manuel Peña."

"How was it working with someone of Liam's caliber for you?"

Ana raised an eyebrow and smiled at Liam, who gazed at her with a cheeky smile. She returned her attention to the reporter, ignoring the swirl of mixed feelings that continued to build inside of her. "Interesting! It changed some of the rules of the game. I had never had to deal with people's curiosity while filming the same way, or the way they inspected me as a person—rather than a director."

"And it was a change in pace for you too, Liam, is that right? How was it different to work in a non-scripted project?"

"It was special in many ways," Liam responded. "It made it feel like I wasn't being filmed, but that might have had to do more with Ana's style and skills, than it not being scripted."

Ana wanted to add her thoughts to that, but the reporter took the mic away. Ana kept the frown away from her face with effort. The swirl in her stomach darkened.

"And perhaps also due to the chemistry between the two of you, as well, wouldn't you say? You look lovely together."

She stuck the mic on Ana's face and the words she'd wanted to say died in her throat. What was the question? The word she said instead brought a soft blush to her face. "Thanks."

The butterflies in her stomach died all one by one.

Liam's professionalism held strong, despite the crack caving inside.

Ana didn't shine the way he thought she would.

The crowd watching the premiere with them cheered when the credits rolled, and people were generous with praise over the film as they all moved to the afterparty. Many of them had also expressed their awe at the rawness of the documentary, and now, as they all roamed around with drinks in their hands, some shared in their own similar experiences.

"I know that shit, man," a local actor shared with them. Liam leaned in to Ana and put a hand behind her back. "Going to Los Angeles for pilot season has taught me some hard lessons."

"Los Angeles teaches us all hard lessons, I think," Ana said.

He glanced at her. She smiled to people around and chatted affably, responding well to the conversation but he knew her well. She was hiding something.

She didn't look up to him, but stared at two people approaching them.

"Hello!" A tall, blonde woman offered her hand to shake. "Congratulations on your film. My name is Marie, and I'm the anchor for the morning show you're booked in for tomorrow. So nice to meet you! This is my co-host, Andy."

The man shot a hand forward. "Hello. What an amazing documentary you created."

"Thank you," Ana said, smiling, engaged; she shook their hands with as much energy as they put in, but her inner spark remained dim.

Mary's eyes were open with excitement. "We can't wait to discuss things with you both tomorrow. Talk a bit more about living in a world that doesn't make room for the person behind the image."

"Yes, absolutely." Liam nodded. "I think it's the power behind Ana's film, how clearly it paints the picture."

"Not living in that world directly, we don't always know, right?" Marie said.

"What I'm always curious about," Andy said, directed at Ana, "is how you handle jealousy. You have to see your boyfriend kissing other people, sometimes even having sex with them and here you are, having to deal with that on top of us nosy reporters, right?"

"Oh no, I'm not jealous. It's his job." Ana shrugged, a strain hidden in her words. "Just like mine is to create these films. I don't think he should be jealous of how closely I get to know the people I work with."

"But you're not pretending to love them, are you?" Andy insisted, a playful smile on his face.

"Andy, tsk." Marie shook her head. "They're professionals."

"I hope you don't ask questions like this tomorrow!" Liam joked. "Ana has no reason to be jealous. That's not how we roll."

"I'll make sure he keeps within the guidelines tomorrow," Marie reassured them. "We really look forward to chatting with you!"

"I'm sure it'll be great," Ana commented and, if Liam didn't know her, he would have believed her.

Chapter Fifteen

ANA LET LIAM OPEN the door to their hotel room for her. Finally away from prying eyes, she allowed her shoulders to collapse under the weight of feigning excitement and affability for hours.

In silence, she took her jewelry off and put it away in its box. Her tired, heavy heart needed a warm bath and maybe a bit of a cry; summoning the little energy she had left, she lifted her arms to her back, trying to reach the hidden zipper there.

"Here, let me help." Liam stood behind her and undid the zipper for her. "You okay?"

Spikes invaded her throat, gripping at her vocal cords until it was difficult to speak. Hot, frustrated tears threatened to trickle up through them, and Ana hated every second of it.

"Not really," she managed to say, stepping out of her dress and hanging it. Mindlessly, she also reached for the complimentary robe there, untouched until that moment, and put it on. She wasn't in a mood to prance around in her underwear, giving Liam ideas. She closed the belt tight.

"I thought so. You've been... off," Liam said.

Off. One tiny, mediocre word to describe the flood of feeling crying to be let out.

"You noticed." She bent down to undo the clasp of her shoes, pulling at the leather straps with rigid fingers. She huffed, seeing red at how the delicate task didn't respond well to the force of her fingers.

God, she didn't like this feeling. She didn't like herself feeling this thing, either. She needed that shower right now to hide until the tide passed. It seemed full of debris, a raising water level that could swoop her up in a whirlpool drift.

Still bending down, face flushed from the position and building anger, she watched him walk by and kick his shoes off from the corner of her eye. She couldn't take this small thing on top of everything else.

Fuck.

She dropped to her haunches, eyes watery, knowing full well that the anger and the tears had very little to do with the damn shoes, and feeling utterly ridiculous.

"Do you need help?" Liam's words came out clipped.

"No. No! I'll figure this fucking thing on my own. Nothing to do with you."

Or maybe a little. A lot.

She clenched her teeth. That was unfair. Mostly.

"Tell me what's wrong." Liam's voice cut the space between them, a rare undertone of irritation in it.

That was a bad sign.

She kept fighting with the straps. Her voice came out grumbly and low. "Don't poke, Liam. We're gonna end up fighting and I'd rather not."

"Do you want some fucking scissors?" He removed his jacket with brusque movements, making quick work of the buttons of his shirt.

She whipped up into a standing position. "Don't."

"Why won't you tell me what's going on? Something is clearly bothering you and here you are, fighting with an inane shoe strap!"

"It's not about the shoe!"

Lips tense, fire in his eyes, he took care of the last button on his shirt, leaving it open as he approached her. "I know that! But you won't tell me what the problem is!"

"I'm invisible, Liam. That's the problem!"

Shit. Saying the words out loud came with the knowledge of them, how real they seemed now that she named her feelings... yet the words shook her, confusing. They seemed accurate yet wrong, and she didn't know what to make of it.

And still it fueled her anger, to recognize the piece of it that rang true.

He unbuckled his belt with the same kind of intensity that Ana had been using for her shoe straps. "You're not."

Now that the first words were out, they all begged for freedom from that place inside her she'd tried to hide them in. Especially when Liam didn't seem to see the part of it that was real.

"I am!" she argued. "Don't you see? They're asking me boring questions while you get all the good ones. All they care about is that I'm your girlfriend, who cares if I directed the damn thing?"

"It is a sad reality that every actress learns quickly." He unbuttoned his pants and took them off. "It sucks, but it's real."

"I'm not an actress, and no one should just accept it, whether they're an actress or not!" She crossed her arms, body tense as she stood watching him. The spikes in her throat were aflame, the heat warming her face and the smoke making her eyes water.

"Then don't take it." Liam turned away to throw the pants over a chair. "You could push back a little."

"Can I? Well, then maybe Becca could have coached me more. She didn't hesitate to tell me what to wear, she can tell me what to say, right?"

He turned around and faced her, no pants, shirt open, hands on his hips. "God, Ana. This is your first time doing something like this. You'll get used to it."

"That's your solution. For me to get used to it."

"So that you can manage it better. Seriously? Don't turn this on me. I'm not the one you're angry at."

"But you have to understand this wouldn't be happening if this were the premiere for another film of mine and you weren't around. But you are, and you might be in the future, and what's gonna happen then? More of the same!" She twisted her hands into fists against her body. "You really need to start helping me out and redirect the conversation somewhere I can actually say something even remotely intelligent."

Liam jerked back. "If I weren't around? That's why you've kept your distance from me?!"

"Really? That's what you're focusing on?"

"Of course I'm going to focus on how my partner keeps on saying things that sound a lot like she's not sure we're gonna make it!"

Ana shook her head as if to clear it up. "What are you talking about? I've never said that! You might not be there for my premieres in the future because you're busy and have your own stuff happening. And it would be different if you weren't there, you know that. You must know that! This is my career, Liam."

"And now I'm talking about us!"

She threw her hands up in the air. "We're in completely different worlds."

"Yes, and that is my problem. Our relationship gets sidelined if your work is on your mind."

Her stomach plummeted to the floor. "That's not fair."

"It is. Last year you almost broke up with me because of your work."

She dropped her hands to her sides, hands in a fist again. "I was never going to break up with you. I didn't even come close."

"But you pushed me away. You're pushing me away again. Do I need to get used to that? Just take it? Learn to live with you saying things like we might be done one day? That when a bunch of reporters ask you dull questions, you're going to avoid me for the rest of the day?"

"Don't take that out of context. You know it's not what I was saying. And we're stronger than that, aren't we? I thought so. I can be angry and frustrated and say things without thinking them through from every angle and it never makes me question the strength of our relationship."

"It's not that simple. Those are not just words. You have to make up your mind, Ana. You keep that margin of error in your mind, always digging at the possibility we're not gonna make it. It grates, right here." He hit his chest with his open palm. "Every time. Did you even realize that, right after we talked about how I'd like to propose one day, you told Logan and Giuliana that you didn't know if you'd ever get married?"

"That's not how I meant it—"

"Do you see us together in your future?"

She stared at him, a gaping chasm in her heart, and she reached to it and stitched the edges together fast, lest it ruin things with Liam.

Her lungs were in overdrive. The skin on her face grew cold.

"It's not supposed to take you this long to answer." Liam's voice rasped out of him, low and heavy.

"I do want you in my future! Of course I do."

Hurt shone in his eyes. "Then why the hesitation?"

"I'm just trying to put my words together."

Ana's heart drummed hard in her chest, knocking against her sternum in a panic. She wasn't sure how they'd gotten to this point, but now that they were here, tears built in her eyes with a warning.

"Tell me the truth." Liam's face hardened, but it didn't hide the raw emotion in his eyes. "Do you doubt at all that we're gonna make it?"

Ana blinked away her tears. "I don't— it's not about that— I think it's just the marriage thing."

"What?" He scoffed. "What do you mean, *marriage thing*?"

Her voice wavered. "Marriage is... definitive. Like— like I've forgotten my heart could shatter."

Liam shook his head. He grabbed at his hips. "So you do have doubts."

"And you don't?! Liam— it's impossible to know for sure. I want you in my life... but I don't know that you will be."

"Why the fuck wouldn't I be? Short of dying—"

"I don't know! What if something happens? Or you fall out of love with me?"

He swallowed a hard gulp, lips pursed. "Is this about your ex?"

"No— yes— no. No. I don't care about Dave, but he proves my point. Relationships rarely last."

He rubbed his forehead with effort. "You'll need to tell me more."

The raspiness in his voice, the mirror of the exhaustion she felt, took her fight away. She sighed, her body dropping the wall keeping them apart in their conflict. The quick stitches in her heart burst open, but she held the wound together, willing it to heal.

She took slow, heavy steps and sat on the settee at the front of their bed. Liam didn't move; he stood in place, body angled slightly away from her.

She sighed. "After Dave and I broke up, it took me a while to even think about meeting new people. Remember *Love in Times of Contempt*?"

"Your film about dating."

"Yeah. I started filming it two months after breaking up with Dave. Part of my grieving, in a way."

He dropped his head and took a deep breath. Shaking his head, he took one of the chairs from the sitting area and placed it in front of Ana, where he sat down. He stared at her, the distance between them colder than it had ever been... his green eyes hardened into emeralds, but he was there. He was willing to listen.

She hoped she'd be able to finally put words to how she felt. "Most people, when they watch that film, see the work that goes into finding love. The constant heartbreak, the low moments when you ask, why bother? Is it even worth it? Only then you meet your person, and you forget all about the bad stuff and throw yourself all in."

He nodded, his eyebrows heavy with his frown. "I remember. That was your question, wasn't it? Why bother? And you answered it by saying, because when it works, it's beautiful."

"Yeah. It's heartbreak until it isn't. Then it'll be worth it."

His breathing came deep yet constrained. It slowly returned back to normal; his face softened, but his frown remained. "Then I don't get it—"

He took one of her legs and placed her foot on his knee. With gentle fingers, he started to work on the buckle of her shoe. That he could be caring in a moment like this broke her heart a little, but love shone in the tears.

She took a deep breath. "I filmed it that way because it was the way the movie needed to be made. But it didn't convince me. Did you realize only one of the people I got in the film had their happy ending? I interviewed twenty people. Twelve made it into the film. I followed five closely. Only one out of all of them found their happily ever after."

"Are they still together? I know you talk to your people a couple times a year—" Liam slid the shoe he'd been working on off, softly guided her foot to the ground, and moved to her other leg.

She tracked his fingers as they easily undid the buckle. "No. They broke up a year after the film came out. They lasted a bit over two years together."

Liam's hands stilled; he brought his eyes to her. "Ana. Just because they didn't—"

"Ely is the most wonderful person I know. Anyone who knows her sees her shine. Yet she keeps having bad experiences, one after another. I made that film because I needed to understand dating again and, you know what I learned? That most of the time, it ends in nothing. Maybe pain. Shit happens. People are used to moving on, these days."

"Sure, some of them move on because they're jerks. Some move on because they're looking for what we have." Liam went back to her shoe, and took it off with ease. He placed her foot down and tilted back to the chair.

Ana's throat closed again with building tears. "Getting together with you last year was all about finding my courage. Being brave enough to risk it and say fuck it, I could be okay with the fear— but I can't say the fear ever went fully away. Last year I thought I'd experienced most of what could go wrong around us, but I didn't. Now I see the true cost. It's been a year and I... I'm here, still willing— more than willing— to take the risk but... when you brought up marriage I panicked a little. A lot. Because it means more than a day at a time— it means I know, somehow, that it's going to work for fifty years."

Liam leaned forward, elbows on his knees and hands linked in front of him. The tone of his frown had changed; he didn't seem frustrated so much anymore, but confused. "I told you. To me marriage means that we may not know... but we're going to fight to stay together. That we see each other as worth the hard work."

"And I want to do that! And I will but I... I guess... I'm terrified of this not working out." Tears filled her eyes. "If this doesn't work out, I don't think I could take it. My heart would break— irreparably."

He sighed. He reached for her hands and held them, big palms warm against her cold skin.

"You know..." Ana wiped a tear away. "Diana gave us a year. She thought we would have broken up by now. It gives me a lot of pleasure that we're still together."

He chuckled.

"And I thought..." she continued. "I thought that maybe in five years I'd build enough strength and time with you to forget this fear... this thing inside of me that tells me it's better to be prepared. Maybe ten. I planned to keep on going until it went away, to be honest."

He smiled and brought her hands to his lips. He kissed her knuckles. "And one day soon— a year or two, so that you don't panic on me again, relax— one day, I want to marry you so that you know I will be here. Until the end. Until you look at me and know I want to help keep your heart in one piece."

"I hadn't realized how unfair it is to you, that I kept that little box inside of me with fear."

"Ana, love... trust in us." His green eyes locked with hers, warm and inviting and confident. "Imagine us at 80, white hair, reading something on the patio... maybe a teenage grandchild is arguing with one of our kids because that's what teens do. That could be us."

She took a deep breath. "Yeah. It could."

"I don't want to get used to you pushing me away. Or pulling away."

She teared up, balling her hands on her lap. "I don't want to get used to that, either. I didn't realize I was doing it. Bad habits die hard."

"My heart would break, too. I know we don't need rings to prevent it but I... I guess I just love the symbol of it."

Ana leaned forward to rest her forehead on his. "I'm sorry, Liam. I know that there's not much sparkle in a director's life. That even though working with you means more people will know my name, no one really *cares*. They still want you. I want to be okay with that. I'm just finding it hard being professionally invisible next to you, while completely exposed as a person."

"Reporters are sexist and they get distracted by the glitter. I thought I was helping by letting you handle them. I know you can speak up for yourself so I thought you would if you wanted to. I didn't realize you needed my help. I'm sorry. And your next project will be all on your own, and you won't have to deal with people like this again."

Ana sighed. "Just... please try to remember to include me in your answers. Give me a chance to speak for myself. And if I'm saying things without thinking that are hurting you... don't wait to tell me. I don't want to do that."

He nodded. "I will. And when my job makes it hard on you in any way, tell me. Ask me for help. Don't pull away."

Ana kissed his temple, his cheek, his lips. "I'm sorry, Liam. For all that it's mine to apologize for. This weekend is far from what I had hoped— we had hoped. First your brother, then these frigging reporters... then me. And a little bit of you."

He smirked, recognizing her teasing.

He squeezed her hands and sighed. "I'm happy to simply be your trophy partner for your next premiere."

She laughed. "That sounds grand. They can ask you questions about how it feels to attend as the plus one."

"I think I'd love that, to be honest."

She looked up at him. "I love you."

"I know."

Chapter Sixteen

LIAM WOKE UP DUE to a tingling arm. Nothing but dull pain would have interrupted his deep sleep. They'd gone to bed late, after fully making up from their first proper fight.

Sometime during the early morning, he'd rolled to spoon Ana, and she'd rested her head on his bicep. Its weight caused the pins and needles running through his skin, but he didn't rush to fix the situation. He pulled her closer with the arm curled around her, and with a firm hand on her soft belly.

"Hm?" The noise came from deep in her throat.

"Come closer," he whispered in the dark room.

"Hm."

She burrowed into him; he sighed. He emptied his mind of thoughts, trying to call sleep back to him, but he failed. His mind raced, going over the events of the previous day, looking for options regarding his brother.

"I can feel you thinking," she said, entwining her hand with his over her navel. "Can't sleep?"

"No." His voice sounded raspy with sleep, just like hers had seemed, both speaking low in the dark.

"What time is it?"

"My watch is next to your eye. I don't want to move my other hand."

She lifted her head to check the time on his wrist, head hovering for several seconds as she likely struggled to see the faint clock hands on its face.

She groaned and dropped her head back onto his arm. "My alarm is about to go off in a few minutes."

"Bloody morning show."

She chuckled against him. "Bloody? How was England, mate?"

"Cheeky wench," he teased, tickling her with the tips of his fingers.

"Don't." She fought his attack by flattening his hand with hers on her body. "I'm too tired. I don't know how you do this all the time."

He rubbed the pliant skin of her tummy. "It'll slow down. It already is."

"Yeah, it is." She sighed.

"So I've noticed something. You haven't been checking reviews and things."

She turned in the bed and faced him. She placed a hand on his chest, eyes still closed. "I learned not to after my second film. I wait for a couple of days before I dive into that."

"How come?"

"I want there to be a bunch so I can have a general idea instead of getting stuck in the details. The first time I refreshed reviews on a loop and made myself sick."

"You're a wise one." He kissed her. "Sometimes."

She opened one eye, its eyebrow high on her forehead. "Ha. Very funny. In any case, Becca is coming to tell us about the first impressions, right? While we're having breakfast."

"Yeah. Nervous?"

"A little." She blinked several times, making an effort to awaken fully.

"Don't be. We'll figure it out, no matter what happens."

Her eyes clear, she smiled at him. She gave him a soft, slow kiss. "I believe that."

———

Ana and Liam waited behind a rolling wall, producers and assistants milling around in the wings. She could hear Marie introduce them to the audience in the studio and those watching at home.

"Ready?" Liam asked. He took her hand in his.

Someone wearing a headset and carrying a clipboard signaled to them— mics were on, the walls would begin to part.

Ana's stomach twisted into a knot; she squeezed his hands twice in response. She hadn't been on TV like this before. At least, with Liam by her side, her nerves were relatively manageable. She nodded to him just as Andy called for them.

"Please welcome our guests, Ana Lira and Liam McMillan!"

The partition rolled to the sides, giving them a view of the stage and the myriad people sitting around it as an audience. The space filled with a mix of applause and vocal expressions of joy, and a feature light shone on them.

Ana smiled wide, hoping she'd struck the right look. She wore her forest-green pencil pants, a white WHAM! shirt and leather jacket, with a bold red lip. Becca had approved and Liam had gotten flirty when she asked about the outfit, and Ana took comfort in that.

Thinking about her clothes was as far as she allowed herself to consider, with the number of people that were looking at her at that moment.

Ana and Liam reached the two high chairs placed on the set for them, as instructed before the show began. Liam offered her his hand, still linked, to help her sit. He made sure she sat comfortably before sitting on his seat.

"So gallant," Andy commented of Liam's gesture. "Polite. You could be Canadian!"

Ana and Liam chuckled— politely.

"Thanks so much for visiting us today to talk about your documentary," Marie said. "Such a gorgeous couple! And that film you created was truly something."

"Thank you!" Ana said.

"This is your seventh documentary, isn't it?" The blonde host checked her notecards, a friendly grin on her face. "Can you tell us a bit about how the content of one of your documentaries depends on who you film? How does that change when you interview someone of Liam's caliber?"

"Yes, it's my seventh film. Working with Liam was serendipitous but not really different than working with my other people. The process itself was familiar. Getting to know him, where he's at in life, how he approaches life..."

Mary nodded. "Maybe that's what makes him more human, in the story you tell us, rather than the superstar that we've all come to know."

"And how was it for you, Liam?" Andy asked. "To get involved in a project that deviates from your usual work must have pushed you in a totally different direction."

"Yeah, it did. I'm used to having a script; I rarely get to use my own voice or choose the words coming out of my mouth. With Ana I showed who I was a year ago and that's a new experience, but let's not forget that I was still directed. Ana is a director— she made it possible to open up and share a piece of me that you wouldn't have seen otherwise. Don't you think so?"

Instead of letting the hosts ask a follow up question, he questioned *her*. Giving her an opportunity to use her voice to give weight to his statement.

She smiled at him and nodded once, hoping he would recognize her gratitude. He did as he'd promised her. "As a director I have two tracks going in my mind, one where I'm asking questions and engaging genuinely, and another that's constantly asking, what are we really talking about? What is the theme I'm exploring here? Because I need to find that connective thread that makes it a story."

"You also produced this film, didn't you?" Andy grinned with such affability it made it clear why he'd been chosen for this job at some point. "Or is this part of the company you have together?"

Ana echoed his expression. "Technically it's part of Jump Cannon Productions— our production company. When we first set it up, it bought my existing company, including the rights for this film."

"This movie really changed things for both of you, didn't it?" Marie waved at them, her note cards an extension of her arm. "We were lucky to watch the film last night for the premiere— congratulations, by the way—"

"Thank you!" Ana and Liam said at the same time.

"— and it's such an interesting film. The contrast between the beautiful weather and the sharpness of how difficult things can be in Hollywood— so stark."

"It's stark in real life, too," Liam said. "There are wonderful, wonderful things about being an actor. There are also rough things, and this documentary was all about exploring those."

"You've said you two were worried about how some people may react to the film," Andy mentioned with a mild frown. "Can you tell us more about that?"

Andy had asked that question to Liam, but Liam turned to Ana to let her respond.

She reached for Liam's forearm and squeezed once in gratitude. "When I met Liam more than a year ago, he was under extreme pressure and it had negative impacts on him. We're showing all of that with this movie and even though we try to make it clear it doesn't deny all the good that comes with it, it can also burst bubbles. The people in my films get vulnerable, whether they're about an immigrant that just landed and is going through culture shock, or a mega star pulled to make more movies. They all show a tender part of themselves and I want to make sure viewers are respectful of that."

Ana gazed at the hosts, engaging with them. Liam put a hand on her thigh, its weight warm and reassuring on her. Stealing a glance at him, she caught the way his eyes sparkled at her.

"That's so moving," Marie commented. She asked Liam, "How do you end up getting involved in a project like that?"

"With a lot of luck," he joked, and everyone smiled or chuckled, including Ana. "I didn't know it at the time, I even fought it a little to be honest... but now I can't imagine where I'd be without this film. It's scary to offer this side of me publicly but I hope it's going to come across as authentic."

Marie nodded. "It does! It totally does."

"And the first comments online seem to agree," Andy added. "People who've watched the film seem to get a good impression of it."

Ana had learned about that earlier in the morning, thanks to Becca. Most early reviews leaned to a positive opinion, with only a few dissident critical comments peppered in for good measure.

Reviewing her card for suggestions, Marie added, "words like *sobering, enthralling,* and even *romantic* are popular in the first reviews of the documentary."

Ana smirked, hiding her smile and stealing another glance at her boyfriend. He returned it, grinning.

"I mean, just look at the two of you!" Marie said. "The film sizzled with chemistry, too."

"She tried to edit it out," Liam joked, "but couldn't do it."

"He flirted too much." Ana arched an eyebrow. "But that's not the point of the story."

"Still another great reason to watch the documentary. Thank you so much for coming!"

Chapter Seventeen

ANA DOZED OFF, IN and out of consciousness as they flew back to Los Angeles. Liam sat next to her, his hand on her thigh as he read.

"We'll be landing in half an hour." The flight attendant's voice woke Ana up, gentle and soothing but clear enough to rouse her.

"Thanks," Liam said.

Blinking fully awake, Ana stretched in her seat. Murmured voices reached her from other sections of their chartered plane; Becca and her team and Mo chatting and laughing.

"Did you get to rest?" Liam asked.

"A bit. Still so tired, though." She yawned.

He intertwined their hands together. "We'll be home soon. Or you will."

"Huh?"

"Are you awake enough to talk?"

"Of course." She sat up and turned in her wide leather seat to face him.

He pushed his lips to the side. "I think I want to go back home and chase Alex."

"Chase Alex." Ana squinted.

"I texted my mom. She said Alex will be home tonight."

"And you want to go talk to him."

He nodded. "Even if I can't convince him, I need to know why he quit."

She leaned toward him and kissed him. "Makes sense. You can take the car; I'll get a cab home."

He sighed, squeezing her fingers. "I want to try to get him to come back."

The cozy warmth of her post-nap state spread within her, a candle flame bursting to light in the center of her chest. Liam seemed to have come to a decision regarding Alex, and it made her smile that Liam's eyes were full of determination now.

"Sounds good," she said, hoping her voice glowed with her desire to support him.

His face softened, and he chuckled. "I thought you might fight me a little."

Smile in place, she arched an eyebrow. "Why?"

"'Cause he's given us trouble already." He shrugged.

"No. I know how much this matters to you. I know that you wouldn't put Jump Cannon at risk."

"If Alex can't make a commitment to the company, for real this time, I won't ask him to come back. But if he can..."

"Then things could finally get going. Maybe you two could actually get better together. And if in six months we come to regret it... we can recoup and change course."

He gave her such a soft smile that her heart melted. "Yeah."

If Alex returned, their production company would have its final set up, perhaps a start to a strong foundation. Liam's acting contracts were finally slowing down, and he could plan for more free time for his own personal projects. Ana had to wrap up this last film, and then could start with their next production—a short interview series that included Liam, and which would serve to network with other figures in their industry.

Checking that no one spied on them, Ana got up and sat on his lap. He smiled, wrapping her in his arms.

"What is this for?" he asked.

She kissed him, again and again, a few brief, sweet kisses. "The future is bright. The film is doing well, Jump Cannon is about to be born, you're slowly getting more time..."

"We're living together and we have the future ahead of us."

"I'm happy, Liam. And I'm happy to have that future with you."

His eyes sparkled, and he kissed her leisurely and long.

"I'm so sorry to interrupt," the attendant said. "But we're about to start descent and I have to ask you to move to your seat."

"Sorry, of course," Ana said.

But they held hands all the way, landing together on the ground as always.

Chapter Eighteen

Epilogue

A YEAR AFTER THEIR life-changing documentary premiered, Ana and Liam got involved in their third project together. Ana's new film documented people who studied hard to pursue a profession, only to stumble into a completely different career. So far, she'd interviewed a psychologist who now wrote romance novels full time, an engineer who'd become a sculptor, and Liam.

Ana had asked him to study the skies and *ponder*, giving him instructions like a seasoned director. She framed him with the Science Center Telescopes in the background; one of his friends from College worked here and it'd given them a great opportunity to film on site. That's what he thought about as he stared at the constellations above him, two cameras rolling around him.

Another thing that had changed since the first project Liam and Ana had done together, was that she had access to better equipment. He knew enough to expect this shot to look amazing on the big screen.

"Done," Ana said. She still preferred to do most of her documentary work by herself, and now she stopped the recording process with a remote.

He watched her check the preliminary results on a screen, biting her bottom lip. He approached her and put an arm around her. "Everything okay?"

"Yeah! Yeah. All's good." She turned the screen off and gave him a brief smile, before turning and going about packing the devices to move indoors, where they were scheduled to film a couple of extra scenes.

He frowned; Ana didn't typically get skittish. He helped her pack and they moved inside into the Planetarium.

Liam loved Planetariums; they reminded him of being a child and asking his parents to take him to Space Museums and Space Centers. He helped Ana set up the two cameras again, one framing him from his side on the seat, the other at a forty-five angle from near the central projector. She sat next to him and checked that she was in the frame but as a clear secondary figure, letting out air in a big, tense exhale.

"You okay?" He asked.

"Yeah! Yeah. Just want to get this right."

"Of course you will."

She put her review device on the seat to her other side and turned back to him, a small smile in place. She leaned forward to kiss him. Her lips were soft yet insisting, and he lifted a hand to run his fingers through her hair.

"Love you, Liam."

He smiled, pleasure overcoming his confusion. "You too."

"Let's do this," she said. "Ready?"

"Ready."

"Do you miss the stars, Liam?"

They talked about his journey to almost becoming an astronomer, and how he made the jump to acting. Liam learned that Ana had managed to interview Julia Hunter, who'd discovered him, but he didn't know what she had said about the moment that changed his life.

After chatting for about an hour, Ana brought the conversation to a close.

"Thanks, Liam. That was awesome."

"Now?"

"Now we watch a Planetarium show together."

The corner of her mouth held a hint of tension but, before he could ask about it, she directed him to lie back and relax.

The light in the room lowered progressively until it became dark, and the show began. Warmth ran in his veins, memories mingling with his present. He flew through space in first-person point of view, his stomach dropping as if he fell into the void alongside the camera, or feeling lighter as he flew faster than the speed of light among distant planets.

The section for constellations began, and a smile split his face. He learned again about the many cultures that had seen shapes in the starry sky, admiring the Mach'acuay of the Incas, the Melipal of the Mapuche, and the Kṛttikā of India.

The journey through the constellations continued with a line connecting unnamed stars to create words out of the fake constellation.

Some folk believed one could see the future in the way the stars journeyed the sky.

Ana moved by his side, likely finding a more comfortable position, but he kept his eyes on the dome. Words faded, to be replaced with new ones.

And some put their hope in the stars.

These faded too, replaced with words that took his breath away.

Liam, will you marry me?

He startled in his seat, hands grabbing the arm rests and tension pinching his shoulders. He turned to Ana, seeking answers.

She stared at him, eyes shining, biting her bottom lip again. She showed him a small box in her hand.

"Ana," he said, voice strangled. "Did you... is this..."

She nodded. She checked the dome and he did too; the words remained shining bright on the dark ceiling. Music had lowered, now a hint in the background.

His heart resumed operations, but his chest had become goo, melted like warm wax, and it struggled to keep up with the rest of him.

"Liam... you said once that you're the romantic one in the relationship, and I'm afraid you were right— I'm not good at this kind of thing and I worried for ages that I was making a mistake. Maybe I'm overdoing it? Maybe you'll be disappointed that I took away your thunder? I don't know." She shook her head. He sat up to come closer to her, but didn't interrupt her.

She opened the tiny box, displaying a silver faceted ring inside. The line of her shoulders straightened, resolution clear now in her features. She continued, "But I wanted to do this. To show you how much I want to make this promise to you, that we'll be together always. You said you wanted to ask me one day to marry you and—" she chuckled— "I really really hope that is still the case. Because I'm here asking *you* to marry *me*. And I really hope you say yes."

Liam's smile split his face, just like his joy stitched him all back together inside of him, even the tiny corners that he didn't know had still been torn and hidden away.

He lifted his hands and cupped her face, staring deeply into her eyes. He saw nerves there but also resolution, and a love as big as the one he had for her.

"Ana, this is a surprise."

"Welcome? Or unwelcome or..."

He kissed her. "You're asking me to marry you."

"Yes. And I'd really love an answer. I won't walk away if you're not ready or if you still want to be the one proposing. Ely is on standby to help me lick my wounds or celebrate, depending on what you decide—"

"Ana."

"What I mean is that I'm not proposing as an ultimatum, of course not!"

"Ana."

"But like I said, because I want you to see just how much I want this with you. I don't want you to ever doubt we're on the same page on this."

"Ana."

"Yes?"

"I love you."

She gave him a smile, but he could see the question in her eyes. "You too. So much."

"I'm so damn lucky to have you. That you would propose to me..." He shook his head and kissed her again. "It's a gift. Slightly inconvenient, for reasons, but..."

"C'mon, Liam. Stop teasing me. Give me an answer."

"I haven't answered yet?"

"No!"

"Oh. Sorry about that."

"Liam."

He chuckled and kissed her again. "Of course I want to marry you. Yes, Ana. I'll marry you."

She melted on the seat next to him, relief on every inch of her he could see. She pulled back into herself, smiling big— such a gorgeous smile— and kissing him once, rough. She took the ring out of the box and held it between thumb and index fingers.

"This ring is for your pinky finger. You use a ring there sometimes, and I thought you could replace it with this one. You and I— and Ely and Alex— know what it means, and anyone else we want to tell... but no one else needs to know until we're ready for people to jump to conclusions."

Grinning, he took the ring he currently had on his left pinky off and, eyes glittering, she replaced it with this.

"We're engaged, now," he said.

They kissed again, and once more.

"We are," she said.

"I have a ring for you, of course. And a plan for how I wanted to propose."

"Oh. Oh!"

"Yes. You beat me by... actually, I'm not going to tell you. A few weeks or months, you won't know until it happens."

"Tell me!"

"No. I think I still want to propose."

"But we're still engaged now. And I'm still the first one to propose."

"You are. And one day we'll tell this story and it'll be sweet."

"I really, really wanted you to know how much I want our life together."

"I do, Ana. I do."

THE END
(but there's a small gift below/on the next page)

Of course I wrote Liam's proposal! If you want to read it, you might want to check out this link:

EBOOK: give me another sweet proposal PLEASE

PAPERBACK: leonorsoliz.com/litoc2ndep or use the QR code below with your phone:

Done And Done, Ely and Alex's story (Enemies to Lovers, Grump/Sunshine, Office Romance), comes next. For more information, check:

EBOOK: check here.

PAPERBACK: leonorsoliz.com/books/done-and-done/

Thank you

THERE'S SO MUCH GRATITUDE in my heart for the lessons I continue to learn in this journey. I want to thank everyone who's walked with me so far, in particular to Mr. Leonor and our little family, for your understanding when I can't think of anything else but plots for my love stories and the one million steps involved in indie publishing. That you understand my ambition and passion means the world to me. And thanks for not complaining too much when I rushed you to edit this story.

I'd also like to thank my online friends, be it from the Council's Chambers, other Discord servers, TikTok, Instagram, or real life friends I keep up with online— thanks for your ongoing support. Thank you so much, Beth, for your friendship and ideas, and for being my beta reader when I've read the story so much I can't understand words anymore. And thanks to Sara, for being such an awesome friend, and for helping me gain confidence in the work I'm doing with my covers.

About the Author

LEONOR WROTE HER FIRST Meet Cute at eight years old and never really stopped. After many years of practicing and dreaming, she took the plunge and wrote a full-length romance novel. Then she wrote some more.

Her stories are written for comfort: love as it can be. Writing love for today means diverse characters with emotional depth and wisdom. Her characters are doing the work, folks.

Leonor is a Latina living in Canada, working as a therapist during the day and fitting as much writing to her life as she can. She's also a multi-crafter, trying her hand at watercolor, jewelry, and anything else that strikes her fancy.

YOU CAN CONNECT WITH ME ON:
www.leonorsoliz.com
hello@leonorsoliz.com
TikTok: https://www.tiktok.com/@leonor.soliz.author
Facebook: https://www.facebook.com/leonorsolizz
Instagram: https://www.instagram.com/leonor.soliz/
Twitter: https://twitter.com/leonorsolizz

Next in Series

DONE AND DONE

Ely and Alex's story. Office romance, enemies to lovers, grump/sunshine trope deliciousness.

Upcoming Series by the Author

BUILD MY LOVE

The story of two Latine siblings and their best friends, and all four of them find their person.

LAGUNA ISLAND

Several interconnected stories with one thing in common: their love for this slice of heaven by the sea.